PENGUIN BOOKS
REMEMBERING LAUGHTER

WALLACE STEGNER (1909–1993) was the author of, among other novels, *Remembering Laughter*, 1937; *The Big Rock Candy Mountain*, 1943; *Joe Hill*, 1950; *All the Little Live Things*, 1967 (Commonwealth Club Gold Medal); *A Shooting Star*, 1961; *Angle of Repose*, 1971 (Pulitzer Prize); *The Spectator Bird*, 1976 (National Book Award, 1977); *Recapitulation*, 1979; and *Crossing to Safety*, 1987. His nonfiction includes *Beyond the Hundredth Meridian*, 1954; *Wolf Willow*, 1963; *The Sound of Mountain Water* (essays), 1969; *The Uneasy Chair: A Biography of Bernard DeVoto*, 1974; and *Where the Bluebird Sings to the Lemonade Springs: Living and Writing in the West*, 1992. Three of his short stories have won O. Henry prizes, and in 1980 he received the Robert Kirsch Award from the *Los Angeles Times* for his lifetime achievements. His *Collected Stories* was published in 1990.

D0953849

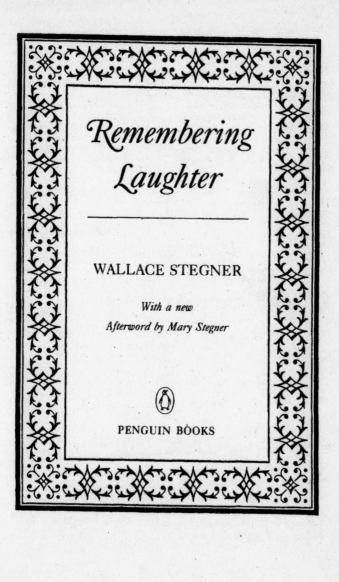

Remembering Laughter

WALLACE STEGNER

*With a new
Afterword by Mary Stegner*

PENGUIN BOOKS

to
MARY STUART PAGE

PENGUIN BOOKS
Published by the Penguin Group
Penguin Group (USA) Inc., 375 Hudson Street, New York, New York 10014, U.S.A.
Penguin Group (Canada), 10 Alcorn Avenue, Toronto,
Ontario, Canada M4V 3B2 (a division of Pearson Penguin Canada Inc.)
Penguin Books Ltd, 80 Strand, London WC2R 0RL, England
Penguin Ireland, 25 St Stephen's Green, Dublin 2, Ireland (a division of Penguin Books Ltd)
Penguin Group (Australia), 250 Camberwell Road, Camberwell,
Victoria 3124, Australia (a division of Pearson Australia Group Pty Ltd)
Penguin Books India Pvt Ltd, 11 Community Centre,
Panchsheel Park, New Delhi – 110 017, India
Penguin Group (NZ), cnr Airborne and Rosedale Roads,
Albany, Auckland, New Zealand (a division of Pearson New Zealand Ltd)
Penguin Books (South Africa) (Pty) Ltd, 24 Sturdee Avenue,
Rosebank, Johannesburg 2196, South Africa

Penguin Books Ltd, Registered Offices: 80 Strand, London WC2R 0RL, England

First published in the United States of America
by Little, Brown and Company 1937
Published in Penguin Books 1996

11 13 15 17 19 20 18 16 14 12

Copyright Wallace Stegner, 1937
Copyright renewed Wallace Stegner, 1965
Afterword copyright © Mary Page Stegner, 1996
All rights reserved

Remembering Laughter first appeared in *Redbook*.

ISBN 0 14 02.5240 1 (pbk.)
(CIP data available)

Printed in the United States of America
Set in Caslon 540

REMEMBERING LAUGHTER

PROLOGUE

THROUGHOUT THE LATTER PART of the morning
buggies kept turning in from the highway and
wheeling up the quarter-mile of elm-arched
drive to the farm—surreys and democrat wagons, an occasional brougham, an even more occasional automobile whose brass caught the
sunlight between the elms. By eleven o'clock
there was a long line parked hub-to-hub against
the tight windbreak of interlocked spruce at
the north and west of the yard, and the house
hummed with the subdued noise of many
people.

Sitting at the parlor window, old Mrs. Margaret Stuart had the whole yard, the drive, and
the highway beyond under her eye. She could
see the white tape of the state road looping over
a low hill a mile to the west, the white gabled
house and high-shouldered red barn of her
neighbors the Paxleys, the cornfields standing

dry and stripped in the thin October sun. Along the road clouds of dust crawled slowly, blown by no wind, almost obliterating the vehicles that raised them. Most of the dust clouds paused at the corner, hung briefly at the end of the elm tunnel, and resolved themselves into the dark moving miniatures of carriages or cars, to draw up at last in the growing line against the wind-break.

Expecting many guests, Margaret Stuart was waiting for no one. There was no curiosity in the eyes that watched the road, no expectancy, no anticipation. A gaunt, angular old woman in black poplin, motionless, hands folded in her lap, she sat before the parlor window and stared quietly out across the Iowa fields and the road and away to the horizon hazy with the attenuated smoke of straw fires.

Seen in profile, she gave the impression of great age. Her face was parchment over bone, with a sharp bony nose, high forehead that rose abruptly into the tightly drawn, lifeless hair, and eyesockets sunk so deeply that they looked at first glance like the eyeless hollows of a skull.

But like many another woman, Margaret Stuart had kept in her eyes the life that had dried gradually out of her body, and anyone at whom she looked directly found himself wondering how he could ever have thought her old. Her eyes were a sudden and violent blue, filmless and clear, and hard as ice. Her body was the body of a woman of sixty, her eyes those of a woman of thirty. Actually she was forty-seven.

The big rooms off the dark parlor were full of people, but Margaret Stuart paid no attention to the sound of many feet, or to the faces that looked curiously in the door. No one spoke to her, she spoke to no one. Elspeth was taking care of them until time for the funeral. There was no reason to go out there now. She sat quietly in the little hard mahogany chair, the rockers never stirring, and stared out across the bare yard and the stripped corn and the road with its rolling cumuli of dust. Outside the great oak at the corner of the house rubbed gently against the shingles, and occasionally a red-brown leaf wavered past the window.

Margaret turned her head as steps came across the bare maple floor of the hall and Elspeth entered. Though Elspeth was seven years younger than Margaret, she looked like her twin. The same tightly drawn hair, the same high forehead and sharp nose with the nostrils bitten in, the same cavernous eye-sockets and ice-blue eyes, the same raw-boned, gaunt, poplin-clad figure. When they spoke, the words of both had a soft Scotch burr.

"Most of them have come," Elspeth said. "The Reverend Hitchcock thinks we should begin."

Margaret looked at the locket watch that hung on a gold chain against the flat stiff poplin of her breast.

"Better wait till eleven-thirty."

"Will you come in soon? They've been asking about you."

"Soon," said Margaret. "Where's Malcolm?"

"In his room."

"Grieving?"

Elspeth nodded. The two were silent, fixed in an awkward stilted tableau, two gaunt black formal figures like identical scarecrows, one standing, one sitting, in the greenish gloom of the parlor. The rockers creaked slightly as Margaret twisted to look at her sister.

"And you?"

Their eyes met briefly, ice-blue and ice-blue, but it was not a cold or hostile look. There was something in it that struggled toward warmth, as if sympathy and affection were fighting to the surface through crusted years of repression and control.

"I'll never be through grieving, I'm thinking," said Elspeth.

The seated woman moved slightly, almost reached out to pat her sister's arm. Then her hands folded again.

"Better get things ready," she said. "I'll be right in."

Elspeth lingered. "How about you? Are you . . . ?"

Their eyes met again, looked into each other across the barrier of bitter years, wavered aside as each found it hard to meet the other on any intimate ground.

In the minds of both rose like smoke the memory of another day in October eighteen years before, and the lips of the woman in the chair were twisted with the bitterness of it.

The noise of many people in the other rooms

was suddenly loud, yet it was quiet in the dark parlor, as if the still air there were a protective cushion against intrusive sounds. Elspeth's hand made a slight silky rustle in the folds of her dress. The oak sawed quietly against the shingles, and three red leaves drifted down in erratic spirals.

"I guess," said Elspeth thickly, "I guess I'd better go see about things."

She rustled out, and Margaret sat still in the little mahogany rocker, her lips tight together, breathing regularly and audibly through her nose, looking out past the burly trunk of the oak at the bare yard and the brittle stripped corn and the road with its clouds of dust rolling toward her husband's funeral.

ON THE AFTERNOON that Elspeth MacLeod was
to arrive from Scotland, Alec Stuart and his wife
were waiting in the town of Spring Mill a full
hour before the train was due. Still pretty at
twenty-nine, Margaret hung on her husband's
arm and walked him up and down the platform,
happy and excited and talking in quick bursts.

Alec, dressed in his best, looking the land-
owner he was, kept his arm stiff for his wife to
hang on, stiffened it still more until the muscles
were ridged and hard when she pinched it in
anticipation.

They were a handsome couple, and he
knew it, and he grinned down at Margaret in
her tight-waisted, puff-shouldered, high-necked
dress, tipped the absurd bonnet perched on her
brown hair. She was tall, but not so tall as he,
and she was slender, and the bloom still on her.

"You haven't been so excited since your wed-
ding day," he said.

"I wish the train would hurry."

"Well, she'll never come the sooner for our walking ourselves to death, my lady. Let's sit down."

"I can't keep still," said Margaret.

"You walk, then. I'll sit down," said Alec good-humoredly.

He sank on a rough bench against the wall of the little station, and Margaret sat dutifully beside him. The town ended abruptly at the tracks, and before them across the few rods of cinders and the double bands of ribboned steel was open country sloping up the long roll of a hill, dark cultivated earth lined with spear-ranks of young corn, white gabled houses half-hidden by flourishing oaks and elms, tufted green woodlots tonguing down through swales, the angles of fences and rutted country roads cutting off black fields from intense green squares of meadow and pasture.

"Think she'll like it?" Alec asked.

"I hope so. I described it as well as I could, but maybe I didn't say enough about the winters, and the summer heat, and the flies, and the like."

"It's a good country enough," Alec said. "She'll like it."

Two men crossed over from the water tank, angling across the street toward the block of stores and shops concealed from Alec and Margaret by the station building. They waved at Alec, and he craned around the corner to watch them. They went in the swinging doors of the Corn Belt Saloon.

"Where'd they go?" asked Margaret sharply. "Into that tavern?"

"Na, na," Alec said vaguely. "They're just walking down the street."

Margaret took hold of her husband's arm again in an almost fierce gesture, as if to hold him beside her by force, but he made no move to rise. They sat for ten more minutes quietly absorbing the spring sun, waiting, Margaret's excitement cooled now by her distrust.

Finally Alec rose. "The horses'll need their flynets, I'm thinking."

While she watched suspiciously, he strolled to the other end of the platform where the horses were tied, and threw over them bright yellow nets of string. Big and casual, he stood there a moment with his hands in his pockets, staring across the street, before he sauntered back to his wife.

"I see Henning Ahlquist across the street," he said. "You wait here a minute. I want to talk to him about working this summer."

"Alec!"

Alec's overacted look of surprise broke down before his wife's look. He tried to laugh away the guilty air that he felt he wore, but the laugh too died in an embarrassed cough.

"I *did* see Ahlquist," he said.

"Maybe you did. But if you go over there you know as well as I do that you'll come back drunk as a brewer, and Elspeth coming in a few minutes. 'Twouldn't be the welcome she'd like, Alec."

Alec eased himself back down on the bench and leaned his elbows on his knees.

"Ah, weel," he sighed comically. "I can see Ahlquist any time."

Half-humorously he studied his wife's face with its little frown and its lips pursed in almost petulant disapproval.

"Why do you drink, Alec?" Margaret's voice

was plaintive, the echo of a thousand repetitions.

"Why don't I, you mean," Alec said lugubriously. "Ye'll make me a drunkard yet, just by keeping me from getting full once in a while."

Looking at each other, friendly again, reconciled, half-joking, they were both aware of the clash of their wills, neither willing to quarrel but with something between them that showed as a pained puzzlement in Margaret's face and an obscure stubborn tightening in Alec's. Alec's stubbornness, his wife thought, was like a rubber wall. It gave, but the more one pushed against it the harder it became. And Margaret's disgust with drink, Alec was thinking, was too extreme. A little nip with a friend was deadly sin. And so they sat with a nebulous cloud of mutual recrimination between them until the whistle of the train announced Elspeth's arrival.

The train slowed for the station, the engine passed them with a prolonged hiss of escaping steam, its iron underparts smoking and its high wheels dragging, slowing, the drivers moving jerkily like a runner's stiff elbows, and before

the cars were completely stopped the two waiting saw Elspeth ready at the door. Then she
was down, running toward them across the
plank platform into Margaret's arms for a long
hug, and out to be whirled high and kissed
roundly by big Alec, and back to Margaret's
arms. There were exclamations and a few tears,
and the smiles of the three were broad and delighted, and then, all a little breathless, they
were walking over to the buggy with Elspeth
rattling about her trip and the things she'd seen,
and the miles and miles and days and nights on
the train, and what a tremendous country they
had here.

As Alec tossed her bags into the buggy and
took her arm to help her into the high seat she
stopped short.

"Ooooh! Your own carriage!"

Alec laughed. Then, solemnly, as he lifted
her in, "I had to get something to haul away the
bodies of Indians Margo and I killed prowling
around the house."

Margaret answered Elspeth's startled look
with a smile.

"He'll tell you more lies in a minute than you

can soak up in a year. Never mind a word he says."

"But aren't there . . . Indians?"

"Not many now," Alec said. "Margo got fourteen with the shotgun off the back porch last year. They used to come around to steal feathers off the chickens for their hair, but Margo's discouraged 'em."

Through the six-mile drive back to the farm Alec was in a constant roar of laughter at Elspeth's questions. They passed several farms with new cylindrical silos, and after the third one Elspeth could no longer restrain her curiosity.

"What are the round things?"

"Wells," Alec said.

"Wells? So high?"

"Artesian wells," Alec said. "They have to be capped or they'll flood the country, and sometimes the water is so strong it lifts the cap way up in the air. Then people have to build up walls to support the cap for fear it'll get tipped a little and fall off the water on somebody. Sometimes they get up two or three hundred feet."

"I don't believe you," said Elspeth. Then to Margaret, "Is he lying again?"

"Alec," said his wife, "stop teasing the child."

"She's no child," said Alec. "She's twenty-two. She has a right to know about things."

And throughout the rest of the ride he devoted himself to telling her about things. He told her of the Mississippi Valley angleworms that were so long a hen worked a whole day to eat one. The hen, he said, would get hold of one end of the worm and start backing away, to pull it from its hole. If it was a really grown worm, that hen would back away from eight in the morning till three in the afternoon, with an hour's rest at noon. When the tail end finally came loose from the hole the worm, snapping together after its long stretch, would knock down trees for miles; and if it happened to slip around a house or a barn, would snap that off its foundations slick as a whistle. Then the hen, if she recovered from the elastic backlash, would start eating her way back toward home, arriving there generally after nine in the evening, dusty and footsore and completely spent, and so gorged with angleworm that she couldn't get in the door of the henhouse.

And he told her of the corn he had raised last year, with cobs as big as the trunk of an elm and kernels like penny buns. It took a four-horse team to haul one of those ears out of the field, and it was a half-day job for two men with a saw to cut down the stalk. And in the night, before it was ripe, the noise of its growing was like a tornado through a forest, snapping and popping and whining till you couldn't sleep.

And he told her about the winds of winter that piled snow thirty feet high over the roofs of houses, so that it took forty-eight hours for the smoke from the chimney to melt a hole through to the air, and when it finally got out it was too tired to rise but lay panting on top of the drifts and froze solid. He promised to show her a stick of it he had preserved in the icehouse.

And Margaret, watching him delightedly pour out a lavish stream of nonsense, watching her young sister with bright eyes and pert disbelieving merriment drink it all in, was contented to sit sedately beside them and let her own

questions wait. There was much about Scotland, about their father's death, about friends
and relatives, that she wanted to know; but
meanwhile Alec was telling about the cannibal
eels in the Coon River, which seeing their own
tails following them, turned and snapped and ate
themselves at a gulp in a swirling eddy of water.

They rolled along the country lane, past
thickets of wild plum, across two muddy, jungly
creeks where the hoofs of the horses and the
iron wheels of the buggy beat hollow thunder
from the plank bridges, over a low hill where
workmen putting up a farmhouse waved at
them, along a stretch of white dusty road to
where the drive turned in between rows of
thrifty young elms that Alec had planted six
years ago. At the end of that elm-lined drive the
two-story white house shone clean and spotless
against a spruce windbreak with the barns loom-
ing red off to the right and the henhouse a long
red bar across the lower lot.

"Here we are, Elspeth," Margaret said.
"Here's your new home."

The buggy stopped on the hard-packed drive before a broad sweep of lawn shaded by two wide-crowned elms as graceful as giant ferns. A cement walk bordered with peonies led to the pillared porch, from either side of which flowers and shrubs spread to girdle the foundations of the house. Elspeth noticed that even the yard beyond the grass plot was clean and well-kept, that it was not, like the yards of most of the farms they had passed, cluttered with machinery and rubbish. The house, too, was bigger, the barns redder, the outbuildings more numerous and in better repair.

Margaret was watching her. "Like it?"

"It's big," Elspeth breathed, "and lovely, and grand. You didn't tell me. I expected a farm. This is a great estate."

They jumped down and followed the luggage-laden Alec into the house. A wide hall opened to the left into living and dining rooms, and on the right a closed door indicated either front bedroom or parlor. Back of the dining room was a huge kitchen where a red-faced Scandinavian woman turned to meet them with flour-coated hands outstretched.

"This is Elspeth, Minnie," Margaret said.

The red-faced woman threw her arms about Elspeth and kissed her boisterously, leaving white tracks on the girl's back. Margaret brushed them off, frowning.

"You should be more careful, Minnie. You'll spoil Elspeth's dress."

"I'm sorry," the hired girl said, still grinning. "I've heard so much about you it was like seeing my own sister."

"It's all right," said Elspeth. "Show me your kitchen. It must be gay cooking in such a place."

"Ya," Minnie said. "Look."

For fifteen minutes she opened cupboards and cabinets, displayed flour and sugar bins, showed stove and oven and pantry, led them outside to the cemented dugout, damp and cool and smelling of smoked meat and storage. Behind the cave was a tiny smokehouse, and beyond that the dark windbreak of spruce and Lombardy poplar. As Elspeth looked, two squirrels chased each other across the back lawn and up the oak at the corner of the house, then out of the oak to the roof, where they sat ten feet apart and ratcheted at each other with flirting tails.

Inside again, Elspeth was shown the two downstairs bedrooms with their tall beds of carved and burled walnut. She examined with a seamstress' approving eye the bright quilt spreads and the dresser covers crocheted in matched patterns of twined ivy leaves.

Everything about the house delighted her except the parlor that opened off the main hall. There, after the light and the bowls of flowers and the comfortable furniture of the other rooms, she was vaguely depressed. The room looked so painfully clean, so formal and unliveable; the sea shells on the mantel looked so rigorously dusted, like a child with scrubbed ears; the walls were so shadowy in the gloom behind the drawn shades; the horsehair couch on which she sat gingerly was so uncompromisingly hard, that for a moment she felt almost like that child with the scrubbed ears, visiting at a strange house with people she did not know.

Margaret saw the look and apologized. "This is the company parlor. I have to keep it closed most of the time, and the shades down so the sun won't fade the carpet."

She walked over and raised the blinds half-way, so that through the window Elspeth could see two men working by the barn, and Alec driving the team down to be unhitched.

Then the older sister came back to sit beside Elspeth, and they talked with Elspeth's hands tight in Margaret's. But even while she was answering questions about how their father had died, and how she had had to live by teaching for almost a year, and saying, "Yes, yes, I'm not lonesome for home one bit," she was thinking: "She's a dear, she's my only sister and I love her dearly, but there *is* something about this room, something about the way Margaret's clothes look so unwrinkled and the way her hair looks as if it could never get out of place . . . There's something in this cold room that matches something in her—it's almost prim, but prim's hardly the word. Prim, starched, stiff, formal, dignified, haughty—none of those. But there's *something*, and it isn't the real Margaret at all, it's only laid on, as this grim parlor is laid on the rest of the house. The rest of the house is really Margaret; but she brings me in here with the sea shells and the drawn blinds and the chairs that dare you to sit down in them. . . ."

Margaret's cool fingers tightened on hers, her voice was soft with maternal fondness.

"Do you think you can learn to like it here?"

"Learn to like it!" Elspeth jumped up as she heard Alec's step on the porch. "I love it already! Let's go up and see my room."

Margaret rose beside her. They were of even height, with the same rosy complexion, the same straight slim figure, the same brown slightly wavy hair, the same bright birdlike eyes. With their arms around each other they went out into the hall.

Pleased by Elspeth's insatiable curiosity, Alec and Margaret devoted much of the next week to showing her about the farm, through sheds and coops and barns, up into the hayloft, almost empty now and smelling faintly of mold and dust, the packed hay in the corners rustly with field mice. Pigeons roosted there, and Elspeth climbed the ladder Alec held so that she could examine a nest with its four spotted eggs.

From the window of the loft they looked out over the gently rolling land quilted with corn-field and pasture, where Alec's Jersey cattle were tawny quiet spots and a Poland China sow with her trailing brood rooted in distant minia-ture. Across the corner of Alec's land the sunken line of a creek was a belt of vivid jungle.

"And is all this yours?" Elspeth asked.

"That and more," Alec said. "I've four other farms, over beyond, that I lease." He waved vaguely eastward.

"The stream is yours too?"

"About a mile of it. We'll walk down if you like."

With Alec and Elspeth swinging ahead and Margaret trailing behind, composedly taking her time and stepping carefully over the rough ground, they went down through the gate of the vegetable garden and out across a field geomet-rically lined with hills of six-inch corn, through a barbed-wire fence which Alec held up for them, across a strip of unplowed land, and down into the shallow flood plain of the creek. On each side of the sluggish stream elms, oaks, cottonwoods, and birch pillared an interlaced roof of branches and leaves so thick that little sunlight pierced through it. Many of the trunks were almost strangled with creeper and wild grape. Cattle trails shouldered through thickets of willow and dogwood, and the black mud of the bank was pocked with deep tracks.

"Don't go near the bank," Alec said. "There's quicksand here that'd swallow a barn. A man fell in here three years ago and his relatives have been putting tombstone on top of tombstone ever since. There must be a hundred feet of granite on top of him by now."

Margaret, who had settled herself carefully on a fallen trunk, shook her head at him with a slight frown.

"Alec!"

But Alec blithely ignored the look. "Fact," he said to Elspeth. "You remember that spotted cow that fell in, Margo? I got a rope around her horns before she went down, and when we got her hauled out she was a perfect giraffe and permanently dry. The suction milked her completely out. Never gave a drop after that."

Elspeth's lips curved and her eyes twinkled at him. "Where is this beast now?"

"Oh, I sold her. A circus gave me two hundred dollars for her."

The girl's laugh pealed gaily among the gray trunks and startled a magpie across the stream into investigative flight. Still laughing, Elspeth watched the bird, turning toward the house to follow it, and saw a man approaching across the sunlit field.

"I wonder if that man's looking for us?" she said.

Alec stared a moment.

"It's Ahlquist."

They walked out to the edge of the timber to meet him.

Henning Ahlquist was blond, slow, powerful, dressed in overalls and blue shirt with the sleeves rolled up, showing huge corded forearms matted with golden hair and glistening in the sun as if oiled. He pulled off his cap with a clublike fist when he saw the women.

"Hello," he said. "I hear you need a hand."

"I do," said Alec. "I thought of you when they told me you'd sold out and sent your family back to Norway."

"Ya, I sold out," Ahlquist said. His voice had the plaintive, chanting singsong of the Nordlander. "I don't want to work long. Just while I get enough money to pay some debts and get back myself."

"Aye," Alec said. "As long as you want, Henning. There's an extra bed in with the Grimmitsch boys."

On the way back to the house Elspeth was silent, watching this huge slow Norwegian with the grave face and the melancholy eyes, wondering what would drive such a Viking away from a land of plenty back to some bleak rocky coast, wondering whether or not he was typical, whether or not she too would want to go back.

"Why do you want to leave here, Mr. Ahlquist?"

The heavy head turned; blue eyes, grave and quiet, searched her face.

"I'm a sailor, miss, a fisherman. I don't like this country."

"Have you been here long?"

"Four years. Four years too long."

In the days to come Elspeth went out of her way to speak to Ahlquist, feeling the loneliness around him, pitying him when she saw him lean

[25]

on a pitchfork and stare out across the growing
corn to horizons shortened by the slow oceanic
roll of the earth. He was like a great unhappy
dog—slow, sad-eyed, indifferent to the people
as to the country around him.

The Grimmitsch brothers—lank, grinning,
tobacco-chewing farmhands—did not interest
her; but this man eaten by homesickness
fascinated her until at times she caught herself
wanting to reach out and stroke his blond mane
as she would have given an encouraging pat to
a Saint Bernard.

Sometimes she would hear Ahlquist singing
around the barn in a clear tenor that matched
oddly with his ponderous size, singing strange
Norwegian songs made stranger by the unfa-
miliar language. Catching him once, she made
him spell out the words, and in her room at
night she wrote down all she could remember
of them, recalling in the quiet lamplight the
melancholy nostalgia of the tune, and the tawny
quiet Viking who sang the song to her completely without embarrassment, watching her
with grave blue eyes:—

Millom bakkar og berg ut med havet
Heve Normannen fenge sin heim,
Der han sjølv heve tuftene grave
Og sett sjølv sine hus uppaa deim.

Ahlquist wouldn't, or couldn't, tell her what the song meant. He only said: "It's just a Norsk song. Fishermen sing it a lot."

And in the dreamful reveries before sleeping Elspeth would imagine the little fishing boats sailing in late afternoon into the mouth of a rocky fjord, with fishermen singing across the black water, and women waiting on shore, and skiffs rocking gently against crude wharfs. At such times she could understand Ahlquist's loneliness; she would lie wide-eyed in the breathless summer night and think, "I'm the only one who does understand him, with his wife gone and his children."

Several times too she took apparently aimless walks that brought her up with Ahlquist where he worked in the field, and he would stop his team and sit quietly listening to her talk, wiping his hot face with a soiled bandanna, and after a few minutes he would cover his glistening hair again with the shapeless hat, shake out the lines, and say "I have to get back to work now, Miss MacLeod," and leave her standing in the rough black field.

Then one day after she had been talking with the hired man while he sharpened a mower blade behind the barn, she came up to the house and met Margaret, who smiled at her reprovingly, maternally, softening the rebuke with smiling fondness but not completely covering the stiff puritan disapproval behind her words.

"I wouldn't be seen too much with Ahlquist, dear," she said. "He's only a hired man, remember, and you've a certain position to keep. People might talk."

"But he's nice," Elspeth said. "And he's lonesome. I think it cheers him up to have me talk to him."

"Yes," said Margaret, as if to a stubborn child; "but he's a married man, Elspeth, and his wife is away."

"Oh!" Elspeth said hotly. "I think that's . . ."

She turned and went out in the back yard, where she threw herself on the bench against the windbreak, thinking furiously how innocent she was of Margaret's suspicions, how Margaret wronged a pleasant friendship with her stiff conventional avoidance of anything that would cause "talk," how she *was* just interested in Ahlquist because he was lonesome. One would think from the way Margaret took it that she was in love with him!

But in her heart she knew that Margaret didn't think that; she knew that this was only what she mentally called the "parlor" part of Margaret speaking. This was only the rural society woman, the style-setter of a county, the rather proud wife of a wealthy farmer who tightened herself up to what she thought her position and built her life on its conventions. In justice to her sister, Elspeth had to admit that the actual suspicion of anything wrong had never entered Margaret's head, and that Margaret had been merely looking out for her respectability. But even so, Elspeth from that time on saw less of Ahlquist.

To compensate for her thwarted interest in the Viking—an interest that still showed itself in greetings and an occasional conversation—Elspeth gave herself to learning about the farm with the abandon of a child. Everything interested her. She spent hours weeding and trimming and cutting flowers with Margaret in the beds that surrounded the house. She took over the daily chore of gathering eggs from the long chicken shed, and every morning the sight of her white dress brought the hens running and cackling to the wire for the wheat she scattered.

The hens amused her immensely. There was nothing, she told Margaret, quite so ridiculous. She could stand for hours watching the stiff, pecking walk of them, the excited scramble when one found a bug, the wandering, aimless search that led them jerkily around the pen.

The imperial strut of the roosters, too, amused her, and she delighted in taunting them aloud—berating them as stupid, conceited coxcombs, putting a hand through the screen to entice them near, and shooing them off with a flutter of her apron to see their suspicious high-toed strut change instantly to dismayed terror and disorderly retreat.

"Poof!" Elspeth would say. "Absurd beasts!" and walk on down to the barn to caress the silky muzzles of two young calves she had adopted, or to scratch between the horns of the placid mothers.

All the animals on the farm the girl liked except one ugly old brood sow which had littered after her arrival, and which two days later had turned savagely cannibalistic, eating all but two of her own young. Every time she passed the pen Elspeth shuddered at the hideous gray mudcovered brute with the meaty snout and the little bloodshot eyes and the scalloped sagging teats.

"Why don't you kill the beast?" she asked Alec, and when he explained that slaughtering wasn't done until fall, and that anyway the destruction of the litter had been his own fault because he hadn't watched her closely, Elspeth burst out angrily: "Your fault? Is it your fault if a mother eats her own children? I could kill that old cannibal myself!"

"Sows do it all the time if they're not watched," Alec said. "Boars too, only they don't very often get the chance."

"Then I don't have any use for pigs, and I won't eat their filthy meat again, ever!"

"You're tender because of the little ones,"

WALLACE STEGNER

Margaret said. "You can't judge animals like humans, Elspeth."

"Why not? A mother's a mother. Even a silly hen takes care of her chicks. I hate that old sow."

Smiling broadly, Alec winked at Margaret, playfully tweaked the girl's ear.

"She's pretty when she's boilin', eh?"

"Oh, you!"

Elspeth flounced out. Watching her thoughtfully throughout the afternoon, Margaret saw her picking tender tufts of grass along the stable wall and poking the green handfuls into the nibbling lips of the two young calves.

A little later the girl was leaning with her fingers hooked into the screen surrounding the chicken pen. Inside the pen the aimless search for bugs and grain was broken suddenly by the amorous rush of a rooster. Hens scattered and flew. The selected victim ducked and scuttled, but at last submitted meekly to her lover, enduring him with a placidity that was almost insulting. Although the rooster pranced a little higher and more pompously for a few minutes, the hen apparently thought no more of it than she did of pecking up a worm.

Elspeth, fresh, high-colored, stood watching, and when it was over she hissed through the wire at the degraded hen.

"You're a disgrace to your sex, you vixen. You've laid too many eggs. Let that pompous dandy treat you so! S-s-s-s-s-s-s-s!" And to the smug rooster: "S-s-s-s-s-s-s-s! You Mormon, you. You Brigham Young! And *so* proud of your-sel'! So ver-ry *ver-r-ry* proud of yoursel'!"

She bent her arms into wings and strutted back and forth outside the screen, mocking him, while the rooster inside watched suspiciously, stopping with one foot in the air, his combed head perking to see her better, ready to fly at the first flutter of her apron.

"Shoo!"

The apron billowed out, and the rooster took off in a stretch-necked run, wings spread, legs desperately pumping. At a safe distance he stopped, adjusted his wings, and resumed his dainty, slow, high-stepping walk, eyeing her suspiciously still.

And Margaret, who had watched the whole thing through the living room window, turned away with a thoughtful face, thinking of the girl's hatred of the cannibal sow, of her ecstatic devotion to the two awkward little calves, of her bright interest in Ahlquist's melancholy expatriation; thinking of the tense fixity of the girl's figure while she watched the rooster cover the hen.

Later, when Alec came up from the garden eating a raw carrot, she met him in the yard. Elspeth was walking slowly down the lane of elms leading to the state road, and the two stood looking after her for some time before Margaret spoke.

"I'm afraid she's lonesome, Alec."

"Na. She has a grand time. What would she be lonesome for?"

"People her own age—boys."

"Boys?"

The carrot stopped halfway to Alec's mouth as he turned on her in surprise.

"She's ripe to fall in love. I've noticed her with the calves, and the chickens."

"What've the calves and chickens got to do with it?"

"Oh, nothing. But I know. I'm going to give a party, Alec. Not just a dinner, but a party. Young people."

"*Um*," said Alec, munching on the carrot, his eyes on the white dress down the row of elms. "I wouldn't go too fast, Margo."

"You think I'm being a matchmaker?"

"Why, it sounds like it," Alec said. "She's met a few people. Give her time. She'll find someone."

Margaret's lips tightened with determination. "I want to give the party anyway. May I?"

Alec hurled the stub of the carrot high and far into the chicken pen.

"Suit yourself," he said.

2

THE DAY OF THE PARTY was sweltering. Heat waves like writhing smoke lifted from the broad fields, buildings from a distance looked distorted and out of line, the red barn blazed with intolerable heat. In its shade half a dozen pigs lolled in a puddle. The cows came up from the pasture seeking the shade of the woodlot, and in the wire coop the chickens squatted in the dust, their feathers spread and their bills half-open.

Even in the house, shaded by its broad oaks, the least movement was the prelude to sticky discomfort. Margaret, miraculously cool and unruffled, divided her attention between supervising Minnie's cooking for the party and keeping Elspeth out of the kitchen. At eleven, when Alec came in from the field announcing that a four-horse team couldn't drag him out there again in this heat, Elspeth was quietly sewing in the darkened parlor. She looked up when his grinning wet face peeted around the corner of the door.

"Would you believe it," Alec said, "the ground's so hot it melted down the disc blades like butter."

"Why didn't the horses' hoofs burn?"

"I shod 'em with asbestos before I went out, but even so they wouldn't stay on the ground. They climbed up and rode the tongue."

"I don't see your shoes scorched any," Elspeth said.

"The heat waves held me up," said Alec. "Just like riding a cloud, but you ought to see the seat of my pants."

They laughed at each other, Elspeth twisting back in her chair to look up into his grinning sunburned face topped by the red hair curly and damp with sweat, noticing hardly consciously the way the muscles of chest and shoulders swelled under the wet blue shirt, thinking him very handsome and strong and amusing.

Margaret's voice came from the kitchen.

"Alec!"

"Coming, my lady," Alec said. He tipped Elspeth's nose with a teasing forefinger and skipped out like a boy when she threatened to throw a book at him.

Margaret took her husband carefully into the kitchen, avoiding touching his sweaty shirt.

"She doesn't know yet," she said with satisfaction.

"How's everything going?"

"Fine. It's going to be a lovely party," Margaret said happily. "Only I'm afraid she'll find out what we're doing and it won't be a surprise."

"It's too hot to work in the field," Alec said. "I'll take her for a walk down by the creek where it's cool. You can keep Henning around to do the heavy work."

"That's it. Then I can get everything ready and put away. Take her out right after lunch."

Alec folded her into a long arm and squeezed her, but she wrinkled her nose at the sweaty smell of him and pushed him away.

"Go take a swim in the windmill trough before we eat," she said.

After dinner she took Alec aside again: "Keep her out till almost six. Then she'll just have time to dress before people begin coming."

He winked and nodded. A minute later Margaret heard his voice in the parlor, and Elspeth's "Oh, yes, it's so hot just sitting here," and then Alec's voice again shouting "You like to come for a walk down by the creek, Margo?"

"Not now," she called back. "You go on. Maybe this evening when it's cooler we can go out again."

Looking through the dining room window she saw them walking down through the garden and into the waist-high corn. She watched them until his blue and her white figure were a quarter of a mile away, moving like tiny boats on the restless green sea, before she called Ahlquist in to move furniture and help in the kitchen.

Because of the heat Elspeth and Alec walked slowly, the sun a punishing weight on neck and shoulders. As they passed between the rows she let the heavy smooth blades run through her hands, stooped to observe the forming ears plumed with green silk, let her eyes range over the green tops stirring in no wind. The rough softness of the soil under her feet, the feel of firm leaves, the wide green ripples of the field, the sense of Alec striding beside her, even the hot burden of the sun on her back, were acute and incommunicable pleasures. She swung her feet out from the soft drag of the soil gaily, crawled laughing through the barbed wire that Alec held up for her, plucked a sunflower as broad as a saucer from its stalk and fastened it in the breast pocket of Alec's blue shirt. And Alec pulled off his hat to make a sweeping bow of thanks, his hair flashing bright copper in the sun, liking the impulsive gaiety of her, a little dizzy with the freshness of her youth.

The transition from the blazing sunlight to the watery green shade of the woods was sharp and pleasant. The furnace of the sky was shut off by a tight canopy of leaves and vines, the hard brilliance gave way to clear filtered light, the soft dry earth of the field was replaced by a softer damp mat of mold.

They sat on a bank overgrown with dandelions and snake-grass, watching the river sliding smoothly like slick brown glass, Elspeth exclaiming as the triangular wake of a muskrat cut obliquely across the stream. Skaters light as air darted about near the shore, and a tanager was a streak of flame against the bright woods.

"The stream looks inviting," Elspeth said. From the grassy bank she stooped to trail a hand in the brown water. "Wouldn't it be nice if we could come down bathing some time?"

"I swim a good bit when I'm working near the creek," said Alec. "But Margo doesn't approve much. She's afraid someone might see me."

"Don't you . . . ?" Elspeth asked, wide-eyed. "Don't you—wear a suit?"

"Na, you can't swim in a suit. Might as well swim in armor."

The girl bent her head in sudden hot embarrassment, dabbling her fingers in the water, pushing a flat palm against the slow surge of the current. The silence between them let in the far caw of a crow from the woods beyond the stream.

"What's the matter with you women?" Alec said finally. "You freeze up just like Margaret at the mention of nakedness."

"No, I don't," Elspeth said hastily. "I don't, really. I was just thinking it was an odd thing to be talking about with Margaret not here."

"Um," Alec said. He studied her averted face. "She probably wouldn't understand. There's a lot of things she doesn't understand. She doesn't understand why I like to tell thundering lies, or take a drink, or go swimming without five yards of wool around me."

Elspeth said nothing aloud, but to herself she was thinking: "I understand. I understand Ahlquist, too, and if I were Margaret I wouldn't be so prim about things." The thought gave her a warm feeling of satisfaction, of tolerant motherly sympathy such as she had felt when she wanted to reach out and pat Ahlquist's blond mane. Now she felt the same impulse toward Alec. Her fingers itched to run through his stiff red curls, and to still the rising excitement in her blood she jumped up.

"Let's walk."

But her excitement did not lessen as they walked. When Alec did not release her hand after helping her over a log, she let it remain in his with a light high laugh and a quick glance at his beaming face. The next time they came to a fallen trunk he put his arm around her and swung her over.

After a time they sat down again at the foot

of a tree. Across the stream a flock of crows
flapped heavily, to settle in the dead limbs of a
cottonwood.

"Let's call 'em," Alec whispered.

He pulled Elspeth down until they were both
hidden behind a bush, threw back his head, and
called raucously, the hoarse caws rasping in his
throat. Elspeth, watching eagerly, saw two
crows rise and sail about as if looking. Then
three more left their perch and climbed shiny-
black into the bright colorless sky. Alec cawed
again. One crow dropped lower, wheeled in
their direction, and after a minute the whole
flock flew so low that the two on the ground
could see their heads bent to search the woods
below. Again Alec cawed. The flock wheeled
sharply and came back. One was just circling to
alight in the tree above them when Elspeth
moved slightly to straighten a cramped knee.
Immediately the crow was off in straight fast
flight, with the whole flock behind him. Their
discordant cries grew thin with distance and
their forms were black specks in the intolerable
brightness of sky before the two stopped staring
and looked at each other.

"You did it!" Elspeth cried gleefully. "They were coming right down."

"I could have got a couple with a shotgun, maybe," Alec said. "Maybe not, though. Crows are canny. You can walk up and tweak their bills when you haven't a gun along, but when you have you can't get within cannon shot."

"Can you imitate anything else?"

"Na. Naught except chickens and turkeys and the like."

He leaned back against the tree bole, puffed his lips loosely, and gave a perfect imitation of a hen who has just laid an egg. Pleased with Elspeth's laughter, he did it again. Then he rose to a crouch, arms bent: scratched industriously in the mold, clucked in his throat, went into a flurry of excitement when he found a grub, pecked viciously at the ground with his nose, swallowed painfully, adjusted his feathers, and strutted off with head cocked on one side looking for more. He transformed himself into a turkey and gobbled so fiercely at Elspeth that she rose and retreated weak with laughter.

Warming to his work, Alec next did a convincing reproduction of a pen full of little pigs squealing for their dinner. He bawled like a cow, bellowed and pawed the earth like a rampaging bull, rushed Elspeth into the brush with a thundering charge. There he caught her and they stood hanging on each other's shoulders strangling with merriment.

"You great fool," Elspeth gasped. "You're a bigger fool than Margaret says you are."

Walking again, they chattered like children on a picnic. At the edge of the timber, on the upper end of the farm, they started a mother quail with what seemed to be a dozen quick, squawking young. Instantly Alec was after them—twisting and turning and dodging, lunging at clumps of weed or grass, thundering heavy-footed after the scurrying balls of feathers. Twice they dodged him completely; then he would circle like a hound on a scent, until one would scuttle from under his very feet and duck into another shelter. Elspeth, standing where they had first flushed the covey, heard him ramping through the willows, yelling like an Apache; then deep and tiptoeing silence; then a whoop of joy, and in a moment Alec came back to her with a tiny quail in his hands.

Elspeth took the bright-eyed trembling bird and felt its thumping heart.

"You frightened it, you lummoxing thing."

"He'll get over it. They tame like chickens."

"Won't he fly away when he gets bigger?"

"Clip his wings."

"*Oo-ooh*, he's a bonny wee thing," Elspeth said. She put the quivering bird against her cheek, and held him there.

When she looked up and saw Alec's eyes upon her, something made her laugh confusedly and turn toward the house.

"Hadn't we better get back?"

Alec glanced at the sun. It was almost five o'clock.

"Let's go back through the trees," he said. "It's longer, but it's out of the heat."

On the way back he followed a little behind Elspeth, thoughtfully quiet, studying her as she walked with the tiny quail held in the hollow of her throat.

Before going up to the house Alec, now matter-of-fact, took the bird from her and put it inside the wire of the chicken coop, where it scuttled for cover.

"Some hen will adopt it in a day or two," he said. "They're very mothering things, hens."

"Hens are nice," Elspeth agreed. "Ridiculous, but nice. You're sure the roosters won't hurt him?"

Thinking of the party to come, of the men who would be there to have a look at Elspeth, Alec answered so harshly that she stared.

"Roosters have no quarrel with anybody but other roosters," he said.

At the front door Margaret, who had been watching through the window, intercepted them before Elspeth had a chance to see into the dining room. She cut off the girl's story of her pet quail and pushed her up the stairway.

"The minister's coming for dinner," she said. "You'll want to look nice. He's a fine young man, and a bachelor."

Having no answer for her sister's arch look, Elspeth went upstairs, and Alec stood looking at his wife's rosy face half-guiltily, as if he had betrayed her. She was dressed in the white gown she had worn the day Elspeth arrived, and she looked almost as young and pretty as Elspeth herself. He let his eyes crinkle in a grinning wink.

"She doesn't suspect anything, does she?" Margaret asked.

"Na. What's this about the minister?"

"He's coming. So is Dr. Van Steenbock, and the Paxleys, and the two Bisom boys, and the Armstrongs, and the Andersons; fourteen altogether."

"Doing it up in style, eh?" Alec said. "But what if she takes to one of the Bisoms? Would ye care for that?"

"No," Margaret said. "But she's got to pick her own. I'm not the matchmaker you think me, Alec. All I'm doing is letting her see them all. Though it would be a shame if she took a liking to one of those wild ones."

"*You're* picking the minister," Alec said with a grin.

"Why not?" said Margaret stubbornly. "He's a good man, and she wouldn't have to reform him out of wild ways. Just because he's not as high-blooded as yourself is no sign he would make a bad husband."

"Maybe so," Alec said. "I was just wondering if he had any blood at all."

Abruptly he went up to his room, and Margaret entered the dining room to arrange bowls and vases on the long white table. As she worked she was thinking that she would have to watch Alec to-night. He was getting restless and rebellious and fidgety again, and that generally led to a drinking bout. The Bisom boys were notorious high-livers, and she had smelled whisky on Ahlquist once or twice, though he never seemed to get drunk. For the first time she felt a twinge of doubt about the wisdom of her party.

The living room and hall were full of guests when Elspeth came downstairs, blushing rosily and surprised enough to please even Margaret. For a moment she fluttered on the lowest step, feeling the eyes of strange friendly people on her, before Margaret came across the hall with regal dignity and led her off for introductions.

The girl moved dazedly from group to group on her sister's arm, trying to fix her first impressions of people into definite mental pictures, trying to remember names and forgetting them as fast as she learned them. Of the first half-hour she remembered only three things:

that the Reverend Hitchcock was a pale-eyed blond young man with very red lips who held her hand too long, that Dr. Van Steenbock was so young in spite of his baldness that she felt a pang of pity for him, and that the Bisom twins' bold stare and assured, rakish manner left her slightly discomposed. The rest of the people were vague faces, sets of teeth, freckles, high white collars, shy smiles, embarrassed grins.

It was not until dinner, when she sat between the minister and the doctor, that she began to sort out her pictures, to match teeth with hair and smile with freckles and embarrassed grin with guillotine collar. The prominent teeth belonged to Mr. Paxley, their nearest neighbor. The freckles and shy smile were the joint property of all three of the young Anderson girls. The embarrassed grin and high white celluloid sat across from her in the person of Jim Paxley, a youth of twenty whose woolen suit and unaccustomed state of full dress made him acutely and obviously miserable. During the dinner he dropped his knife on the floor with a clatter, stooped to pick it up, and came back up above the table edge with the uncomfortable grin stuck with dreadful permanence on his purple face. Sight of so much distress gave Elspeth enough poise to let her feel comparatively at ease. She was able, having located a few land-marks, to pick out others—Mrs. Paxley, large and many-chinned and beaming, slightly out of place, as her son was, in a social gathering; Johnny Armstrong, snub-nosed and mildly vin-egarish, sitting next to his snub-nosed and vin-egarish sister; John Anderson, full of the dignity of years and membership in the State Senate, and his slim birdlike wife caged in ecru lace.

As her embarrassment left her, Elspeth found the guests very affable, very friendly, very com-plimentary with looks and words. John Ander-son joshed her heavily about the strong probability that she could pick up a model hus-band out of such a gathering of the country's eligible bachelors, whereupon the Bisom boys grinned knowingly at each other, the minister wet his red lips, the doctor's skull grew vio-lently pink, and Jim Paxley choked on a mouth-ful of chicken. The saturnine Johnny Armstrong stared coolly at the Senator, and Alec, at the head of the table, looked down the linen length of it at his wife, who squirmed a little and began talking gowns with Mrs. Paxley, who knew rather less about gowns than a Digger Indian.

Once or twice during the dinner Elspeth glanced up to find Alec's eye on her, and at such times she was painfully aware that the minister in his eagerness to talk bent almost over her plate while torrential words rushed from his wet red lips. It made no apparent difference that most of the time she was turned toward the doctor, who did not embarrass her as the other did, and whose hairlessness insured her respect. The minister still talked, bending farther to catch her attention, and Elspeth, swinging from doctor to preacher and back to doctor in order to be polite, would look up to see Alec's lips curl contemptuously, and the flush would creep again into her temples.

Somehow, during the hectic dinner, she learned that the doctor was a Dutchman born who had been brought to America at the age of six and had studied at Harvard; that the Reverend Hitchcock was of old New England stock, had studied at three different seminaries (there was a flavor of pride about this, she felt),

WALLACE STEGNER

that he was all alone here in this Western state
and was lonely—yes, it was lonely here for cul-
tured and educated folk. Didn't she find it so?
She learned, though she couldn't have told from
whom, that the Bisom twins were the sons of
an Englishman who owned even more land than
Alec, up north of Sac City; that their father had
made of his farm an English estate, had im-
ported foxes and hounds, and rode on the hunt
every week with his two swashbuckling sons.
She learned that the Andersons were comparatively wealthy people blessed (she mentally put
a mean question mark after the "blessed") with
three unattractive daughters. She guessed that
the Paxleys had been invited because they were
newcomers and neighbors. Of the Armstrongs
she heard nothing, but they too were obviously
well-to-do, part of the county aristocracy. Even
while she was still slightly ruffled at being
plumped suddenly in the midst of all these
strangers, Elspeth could smile a little, inwardly,
at the assumption of aristocratic position which
they wore. Of the lot, she thought, Margaret
was the only aristocrat.

After dinner, while the older people sat com-

fortably about the walls, there were games., By
now Elspeth had shed her confusion, and gig-
gled excitedly with the Anderson girls as they
walked warily around the circle of chairs playing
"Going to Jerusalem." All the unmarried people
played, even the Reverend Hitchcock, but Elspeth noticed that by some means or other one
of the Bisoms was always next to him, and always shunted him urgently away from the chair
he leaped for at the signal. In four games the
minister was always the first one out. Jim Paxley
was next, again through the agency of a Bisom.
After that the Bisoms and Johnny Armstrong
and the doctor struggled for chairs with the five
girls, and the laughter of players and spectators
rang through the long room. There was much
bodily contact, much pushing and argument
when two people each got a precarious seat on
one chair. On the sidelines with the "outs" the
Reverend Hitchcock wet his red lips and pursed
them in agitation as Elspeth and the doctor
fought for a seat and the doctor's arm went
around her in the scuffle, or when one of the
Bisoms, who were exasperatingly indistinguish-
able, grasped the girl's shoulders and whirled

her gasping out in a wide circle to land on his
lap in a shout of mirth.

Then in the panting interim between games,
while the boys mopped their brows with con-
spicuously white handkerchiefs and the girls
fanned hot faces, one of the twins proposed
"Post Office." The minister pursed his lips
more strongly. The group of young people grew
quiet, eyes turned toward Margaret. "Post Office" in the presence of the minister was pretty
daring.

"Do you think it would do any harm?" Margaret said weakly. She wanted the party to be
gay, she wanted Elspeth to have a good time,
but "Post Office" . . .

"I cannot, of course, approve," said the Reverend Hitchcock. "But I am only a guest. I
would not think of censoring anything in my
hostess's home."

He almost bowed. Out of the cluster of waiting boys and girls came a *sotto voce* "Oh, rats!"
that sent a titter through the room.

Alec rose from his chair grinning.

"Come on," he said. "We'll all play except
those who disapprove. Come on, my lady."

He held a hand out to his wife, but she remained seated with a slight frown and a shake of the head, and while the game went on the martyred defender of decency drifted over to stand by her watching intently, his tongue flicking out to wet his red lips and his eyes alert behind the glasses. Both he and Margaret noticed that one of the Bisom boys seemed always to be kissing a girl, generally Elspeth, and that they frequently fudged and stole kisses they were not entitled to. The little tight frown stayed on Margaret's face. The doctor, bald and pinkly shining, was worse than useless in such competition, and Alec, who might have had the grace to help, was delightedly bussing his victims with exaggerated clownishness, elaborately unaware of his wife's attempts to catch his eye.

At the very height of the game, when giggles and guffaws of triumph and squeals of simulated terror echoed through the house and quivered in the long slack curtains, when the game had degenerated into a pursuit-and-capture formula, Margaret rose abruptly and went to the piano. Over the heads of the party floated the strains of "A Bicycle Built for Two," and Larry

Bisom swung the girl he was kissing at the moment off in a wild polka. Other couples joined the dance, but Alec and Elspeth, with a covert glance at each other, both sheepish now after their defiance of Margaret and the minister, went to the piano and stood there singing.

Again the Reverend Hitchcock joined them, and before many minutes was standing with his arms flung, as if carelessly in the abandon of song, over the shoulders of both Margaret and Elspeth.

"I wonder you're not out stopping the dancing," Alec said.

"Dancing," said the minister, "is, if properly conducted, a refined and entertaining exercise."

He offered his arm to Elspeth, who, unable to refuse, followed him in a stiff waltz while Alec glowered and Margaret, looking up over her shoulder, smiled at her husband with a hint of malice and nodded as if in time to the music she was playing.

After a time Margaret was relieved at the piano by one of the Anderson girls anxious to show her talents, but when she looked for Alec he had disappeared. The dancers had blown vigorously at the banked candles on mantel and sideboard, and the rooms were only dimly lighted. A careful count of those present left Alec and both Bisoms still unaccounted for. In growing apprehension Margaret sat down in the dark parlor and watched the dancers swing by in the hall, waiting to see if the three would come back, surer every moment that they would not. She knew Alec, and she had heard a great deal about the Bisom twins.

At eleven o'clock Alec had not returned, and Margaret's uneasiness had become fidgety certitude. When Paxley, red-faced and beaming, pranced by with Elspeth, Margaret motioned to her sister, smiled an apology at Paxley, and drew Elspeth over to the stairway.

"Have you seen Alec?"

"No," said Elspeth. "Not for almost an hour. He went out somewhere. He didn't seem to like dancing much."

"Stuff!" Margaret said, flushing. "He loves dancing. He's . . ."

The words stopped themselves on her tongue.

"Would you sit with the minister awhile?" she asked. "I'll go find him."

"Oh, no," Elspeth said quickly. "Don't disturb yourself. I'll find him. I need a breath of air anyway."

She pushed her sister back into the parlor, waved an "I'll be back" which she didn't mean at Paxley, and went from the hot hall into the warm night air, relieved to be out of the stuffy uproar, pleased with the ragged moon just showing over the corner of the barn.

Finding no one on the lawn, she walked toward the black bulk of the barn, and with the abruptness of stepping from land into water, passed from the moonlight into the clean-edged rufous shadow. Above her was the sharp thrust of eaves against the pale sky, and before her the feel of wall, a more solid shadow than that on the ground. Somewhere ahead was the low mumble of voices.

Feeling her way around the wall, the girl passed the corner, was immersed again in moonlight that made the folds of her white muslin shimmer blue as she moved. The voices were louder now, and a square of dirty yellow low down in the end showed her where they came from. In a moment she stood uncertainly outside the window, shivering a little with the night air now that her blood had cooled.

Through the smeared pane she saw Alec and Ahlquist and the Bisom boys sitting around the low table in the harness room with a bottle before them. Their voices seeped through the wall in a deep masculine rumble.

Elspeth's indecision grew. The prospect of interrupting four men at a drinking bout, even though one of them was Alec, was terrifying, but her impulse to turn back was smothered before she had taken a step by the thought of Margaret fretting and worrying in the house. None of these men would hurt her. They could go on drinking till they fell under the table after she got Alec away.

Firmly she pulled open the half-door and stepped into the black interior heavy with stable smell. The door of the harness room, a few inches ajar, laid a guiding finger of light down the three wooden steps, and up these she climbed, walking heavily to give the men warning. Before she knocked she heard the swift exclamation and sudden movement inside, the abrupt cessation of their voices, then the sound of her own knuckles on the boards, so thin and timid that she was ashamed, and Alec's "Come in," in answer.

The girl pushed open the door and remained in the doorway, seeing in a quick glance the confusion behind the Bisoms' grins, seeing Ahlquist's slow nod, the grave, sober look on his face, noticing as significant the alacrity with which Alec jumped up. The bottle was nowhere in sight.

"We were just talking over crops," Alec said lamely. "The party isn't over, is it?"

"No," Elspeth said. "Margaret thought you should come up to the house."

Immediately she felt guilty, as if she had given Margaret away for a suspicious wife, and that guilt, plus the feeling that she had been eavesdropping, made her turn and stumble down the steps to the moonlit barnyard.

Alec followed and stood beside her, his big

body black beside the frail white of her gown, his hair tousled and glinting in the moon, the reek of whisky strong upon him.

"I'm sorry," Elspeth said.

"Never mind. Margo sent you, eh?"

"Yes. She thought you'd been . . . drinking."

Alec ran a hand through his hair with a hard little laugh.

"I have," he said.

Automatically they started walking toward the house.

"Why?" Elspeth asked.

The idea that Alec did not like the party, that there had been some reason for his leaving so abruptly, would not down. And below that idea, in some substratum of consciousness, was a feeling that was hardly so much a feeling as a premonition, a hidden, tingling intuition that she herself was somehow involved.

In the shadow under the eaves Alec's hands grasped her shoulders roughly, swung her around to face him in the dark.

"Why?" he rasped. "I'll tell ye why, Elspeth. I couldn't stand that crew looking ye over. If

I'd stayed in there a minute longer I'd have smashed that preacher's prissy face. It's too much like putting ye up on a table and taking bids."

Uncomprehending, Elspeth shrank under his rough hands, stammered. Yet when he pulled her close to him, swept her into a tight embrace, she yielded limply, gave her mouth to his furious kiss.

Alec released her so sharply that she staggered. In the shadow she could not see his face, but when his voice came she knew that he was not apologizing.

"I've been wanting to do that for a month," he said.

Elspeth moved closer to him, driven by the guilty shadows, feeling her whole world fray out in love and shame.

"I . . . Oh, Alec!"

Her need rose in her like hot tears, and the moment of their intimacy lengthened into minutes while the creeping moon narrowed the belt of shadow in which they stood and the sound of the piano rose and died through the open doors and windows of the house.

"Margo wanted to give this party so you could find yourself a man," Alec said.

"Poor Margaret!" Elspeth said. And then, shivering close against him, "Poor Alec! Poor Elspeth!"

3

WHEN ELSPETH AWOKE next morning that moment in the shadow of the barn was like something she had dreamed, an image that lurked on the troubled borders of memory, and the meeting with Margaret at the door appalled her with its implications. Margaret straight, quiet, deeply hurt; she and Alec humbled by their sense of treason; the beauty of the moment gone as light goes, and only their shame left . . . Margaret's quiet "You'd better go to bed," to Alec, and Alec's "Right, my lady," and afterward the task of smiling "good night" to departing guests; and then the intolerable minutes sitting with her sister on the horsehair in the parlor, while Margaret's grief at Alec's actions came out of her in disjointed, restrained, tight-lipped words that tried vainly to break through Elspeth's half-hysterical defense against being a confidante . . .

"I can understand Ahlquist," Margaret had

said. "His family is gone, and he's lonely, and he misses his country and people. But Alec hasn't that excuse."

And Elspeth, knowing from that brief revelatory intimacy in the shadow the incommunicable excuses Alec did have, sat stiffly on the stiff couch beside her sister hating Margaret but hating herself and Alec more. A few hours earlier they had all been grand people, she thought unhappily, grand people happy in each other's company, none of them with any ill-will or intention of wrong. Now they had suceeded in so tangling the threads of their lives that only misery could come of it.

For a long time the girl lay quietly in bed, watching a squirrel tight-rope the eaves outside her window, thinking of that kiss in the shadow of the barn and what it meant, trying to bring those disquieting five minutes into focus, reduce them to scale with the rest of her life, repeating over to herself that neither Alec's action nor her yielding had any meaning, telling herself that he had been heated with whisky and that she had been excited by the party, by the dancing and music, by the laughter and the kissing game. The kissing game . . .

When she had argued herself into the belief that the whole night had been merely a passing incident without significance, and had finally dressed and gone downstairs, Margaret had her breakfast waiting. Alec was in the field with the men.

While Elspeth ate without appetite her sister came over to lay a hand on her shoulder.

"I'm sorry your party ended so badly, dear."

"Don't be!" Elspeth said in a burst of contrite affection. "Please don't be. It was a lovely party."

And later, helping Margaret and Minnie straighten the house, she resolved that at noon she would talk to Alec, tell him that the evening before was a fiction, that she had been foolish and was sorry, that he must not think it important or lasting.

But when Alec came in he avoided her eyes, ate with his eyes on his food, said a few monosyllabic words, and escaped from the constrained table. It was three days before Elspeth could corner him to tell him what had become an increasingly fierce monody in her mind.

They met at the chicken pen, Elspeth with her apron full of wheat for the chickens, Alec with a sack of corn for the hogs. He set the sack on the ground and stood silently beside her as she scattered the grain, and she, without turning her head, felt him as an almost sinister presence, so that her voice cracked a little on the clucking *"Choo-oo—ook, chook, chook, chook!"* and she took a very long time carefully casting handfuls to her pet quail which now ran and pecked with the chickens.

"I told you he'd tame," Alec said.

Elspeth's hands shook out her apron, and then went behind her as she turned to lean against the post and look up at him, fright now upon her as her determination weakened.

"I wanted to tell you . . ." she said, and stopped, furious at the unconvincing weakness of her voice. *He won't believe me*, she thought, *he'll think I'm lying, that I really love him and am afraid*. She blushed hotly, and was furious at that too, but her voice steadied.

"We weren't fair to Margaret the other night. You were drunk and I was foolish. Of course it didn't mean anything, but I wanted to tell you —so you wouldn't . . . think . . ."

Her words trailed away to nothing, and under

her lashes she looked up at him, ready to laugh with him and forget it at his word and find herself back on the old friendly ground. But the serious stare of Alec's eyes disconcerted her again. He was not ready to laugh. He was not going to say the word. He wasn't going to let her out.

"Ye're faking," Alec said soberly. "It's no use, Elspeth. When I said I'd been wanting to do it for a month, I meant it. It's no good hiding your head in the sand."

Without answering, terrified at the weakness she felt in herself, the girl turned and ran down to the barn. Alec picked up his sack, emptied it in the hog trough, and followed her slowly, his lips stubborn and a hard vertical wrinkle between his eyes.

He found her with her arms around one of the pet calves, crying into its sleek neck. With a quick look to see that the stable was empty, Alec put his arms around her and pulled her against him, kissed her wet face. As before she clung to him, cried for a few minutes against his shoulder, and then, without a look or a word, pulled away and left him.

And Alec, with a pat on the calf's flank that began as a caress and ended as a blow, went out the other door of the barn.

After that experience of how little strength her resolves had, of how smoothly she could be betrayed by her feelings, and knowing also that Alec's stubborn refusal to hide what he wanted might lead to a disclosure of what she took to calling "the whole silly shameful business," Elspeth kept strictly to a program of chaperonage for weeks. She took long drives with Margaret, or with Margaret and Alec together, but never with Alec alone. When she walked, she walked by herself, refusing herself the company even of Ahlquist because Margaret had shown disapproval of that.

During these days she acquired a hard bright gaiety that was able to talk and joke with Alec in Margaret's presence, but that left her instantly when there was danger of their being alone. Her defenses turned the least word of her brother-in-law into a jest, parried his subtlest advances, reduced him to moody silence.

When September drew on and the blades of tall corn began to dry yellow, and when the ears grew heavy and hard, there were extra hands to feed, threshers and huskers and teamsters; and she threw herself into preparing food for these men with an industry that more than matched Margaret's cool efficiency and Minnie's oxlike capacity for work. She went to the field and made Ahlquist show her how to husk corn, and many afternoons she worked down the long rows with the men, loving the hazy sunlight and the sense of heavy harvest, hands and feet moving rhythmically to the sound of cobs against bang-board, drawing healthy enjoyment from the creak of harnesses and the tinkle of bits and the dusty sneeze of the horses, laboring mightily to leave a clean row and still keep up with the men. And Alec, watching her go down the rows stripping out ears and tossing them into the trailing wagons, said nothing. When Margaret complained that Elspeth was killing herself needlessly doing a man's work, he only grunted and said that she knew best what she wanted to do.

Twice after the party the minister called on

Elspeth. The first time he cornered her in the parlor and held her in talk for two hours, leaning over her eagerly, holding her hand until she pulled it away, telling her of his struggles to set up a house of God in the wilderness, the indifference of many of the people, the lack of educated companions, the loneliness of his life. He regretted a thousand times, licking his red lips with a quick tongue, that they did not live in his parish so that he could have the joy of their support and company, and at the end of his two hours he departed, leaving her weak and slightly nauseated.

The second time he came Elspeth was working in the field and came up in answer to Margaret's call, drawing off her heavy gloves and kicking the dirt from her shoes, her clothes dusted with the yellow powder of husking. She was feeling especially alive and quite happy, but the sight of the minister's buggy in the drive stopped her at the edge of the barn.

A quick glance showed her neither Margaret nor the preacher in sight, and on a sudden mischievous impulse the girl ran across the intervening yard, untied the horse, leaped in the buggy, and was off down the lane to the state road. She was a hundred yards away before the two got to the door, and then she blithely waved at them and continued down between the elms, ignoring the Reverend Hitchcock's dismayed shout and Margaret's shrill "Elspeth!"

This time, she thought gaily, he'll not keep me listening to his gabble for two hours! Let him visit Margaret! And so she drove slowly out along the road, stopped at Paxley's for a drink and for the pleasure of telling what she had done to the preacher, took Jim Paxley away from his work and out for a fifteen-minute spin, loitered back past the Stuart lane and on down toward Sac City a mile or two, and finally, when she judged that enough time had elapsed, drove back to the lane and up the drive.

Margaret and the minister met her at the door, and she sat in the buggy seat keeping her face straight, waiting for the reprimands.

"I can't imagine what's got into you, Elspeth," Margaret said. "Reverend Hitchcock drove all the way out here to see you, and you steal his horse and go driving."

"I didn't know he came to see me," said Elspeth. "I thought he came to see you, and I didn't think he'd mind my using his buggy. It would be pretty small charity that would begrudge a girl a few minutes' rest from hard work."

She pulled her heavy work gloves back on and stepped down to face the preacher's trembling insultedness. With a visibly tremendous effort he swallowed his rage and hurt pride and essayed a mild rebuke.

"You shouldn't try to work in the field like a man, Miss MacLeod. Farm girls, yes; but not you. You're not a farm girl. You're a young lady. You should grace a parlor, or lighten a good man's home."

"Oh," said the girl airily, "I like working like a man. It's great fun. You ought to try it sometime."

When the minister had climbed to his buggy and flapped the lines across the back of the horse and had rattled down the drive and out of sight, Elspeth dropped her airy innocence and touched Margaret's arm.

"I'm sorry, Margaret, but if I'd had to talk to him for two hours again I'd have burst. He makes me feel as if I had bugs crawling all over me."

"Well," Margaret sighed, "I doubt if you'll be bothered with him any more. You succeeded in insulting him very thoroughly."

"I meant to," said Elspeth.

By the time Indian Summer dropped its warm haze over the stripped fields, and the oak and sumac were crimson in the woods, Elspeth had come to believe that everything was right again. Alec had made no advances. Perhaps, she thought, he has forgotten, perhaps I can relax, perhaps the shell can be sloughed and I can be me again. She found that she could talk to him naturally and with the greatest friendliness at dinner or over the whist table. She could cling to his arm with never a secret fear of her own weakness, never a silent thought that she wanted him to be otherwise than friendly, when they walked down through the autumn woods. She could chatter like a magpie at the incredible crimsons of the leaves or the broad fields of late sunflowers, and she could sail milkweed pods with him while Margaret sat on the bank smiling and composed, even her walking clothes reflecting somehow her flair for the immaculate.

The perfect weather of Indian Summer lengthened and lingered, warm sunny days were followed by brisk nights with Halloween a presentiment in the air. In the afternoons the smoke of straw fires was blue on the horizon, and the lawn before the house was thick with crisp leaves.

On such an afternoon Elspeth was moping about the house, wishing that someone would call, even Jim Paxley. With the harvest hands gone there was little to do and no one to see. Alec and Ahlquist were taboo. The minister had not called since the stealing of his buggy. The Bisom boys, who had ridden over occasionally in August, were now in Omaha, she had heard. Dr. Van Steenbock was busy with his practice in town and had not visited them since the party, though every time they drove in they met him and had his blushing promise to come out the first time he got a free moment.

Elspeth tried sewing, but restlessness made

her stitches hurried and impatient. She hunted for something to read, but all the books in the house were stale, and Margaret's new batch of fashion magazines would not arrive for another week. At last, as she had done a dozen times before, she wandered outdoors for a walk, down past the chicken pen where she stood for a while watching her quail. But she felt little interest in the bird any more, now that it was tame and unafraid. It was, she decided, a rather dull fowl, little better than a guinea hen and just as stupidly domesticated.

A little below, the vicious old brood sow lay full length dozing in the trampled mud of the sty. As the girl passed, the sow reared upon her front legs, her heavy hind quarters dragging, and stared out of little red eyes, the rubber snout moving, water glistening on meaty shoulders and straight legs.

"You ugly brute," Elspeth said. "In about a week now you'll be slaughtered for your pains, and I'll be glad. You hear? I'll laugh when they cart you away to market, you cannibal you."

She was now definitely on her way to the creek, though she had had no intention of going that way when she started out. And in the sere field, where pumpkins shone orange among the stalks, she felt better. Her body was lighter and freer, her ears caught the papery rustle of the dry blades of corn, and ahead the thinning red and gold of the timber was still vivid enough to bring anticipations of scuffling feet in knee-deep brittle leaves with the quiet of the woods and the water around her, and squirrels nutting, and robins thick on their way south.

By the time she reached the woods the girl had lost all her dullness. She whistled at the squirrels, threw them acorns and hickory nuts, laughed delightedly at the undulant grace of their tails. Many times she stopped breathlessly in the crinkling leaves to watch flocks of robins and flickers, or to observe a redheaded wood-pecker drilling for an insect. Later, Margaret had told her, the robins would be gone, and all the other birds except the crows, and then the jays would come by on their migration, to fill the air with their clamor for a few hours and vanish. After the jays had come and gone, there would be winter.

Elspeth sat finally on a heaped pile of leaves

by the river, and muskrats swam close with their bright button eyes and whiskers above the water, with the suggestion of strong unseen muscular effort in the way they swam, and the long triangular wake streaming out behind to be bent and strained and finally broken by the slow current. The motion of an arm to toss a curling maple leaf in the water, and the swimmers vanished in a swirl of smooth brown. Sometimes she counted thirty before they came up again rods away from where they had dived.

Elspeth was sitting quietly, full of a still peacefulness, but stirred too by her old restless desire for activity, loving the autumn woods but hating the prospect of long winter days cooped in the house, rebelling with a slow surge of feeling, still only half-felt, against something she couldn't have named, when Alec, coming through the woods with a strayed calf, discovered her.

Without speaking, Alec took the rope from the neck of the calf and shooed the animal into the field toward the house. Then he sat down by her in the crackling leaves.

"You found a nice spot."

"Lovely," Elspeth said. Her pulse was still racing from the start he had given her. "I couldn't stand it in the house any more, so I came out for a walk," she said.

For a long time they were so still that a swimming rat approached within fifteen feet, but swerved suddenly and dived when Alec's head came up to see if Elspeth was watching it too.

"Remember when we called the crows?" he said.

"I was just thinking of it. The wild ones don't seem very afraid of us, do they?"

The old unnameable reckless impulse was rising in her again, to be snubbed short by the old terror at herself. Alec saw her hand shake as she reached out for a leaf to toss into the stream, and he caught the hand before it could throw.

"Elspeth!"

And with only a momentary struggle, like the hidden underwater effort of the swimming rat that showed only as a kind of strained intensity in its moving head, the girl yielded and the watchfulness of more than two months went out like a child's mud dam. She felt his fingers bite into her arms, felt her body broken backward and his hand fumbling at her dress, felt the hot shock to her blood as his calloused palm touched her breast.

The half-grown calf, freed from the rope around its neck, browsed off into the yellow field, nibbling at fallen ears that the gleaners had missed. From the woods beyond the stream came the far derisive caw of a crow.

A half-hour later Alec and Elspeth followed the calf, Elspeth clinging tightly to her lover's arm. Their stiff silent march to the house was somehow a penance, a walking barefoot over hot coals, a march to the gallows. *We're both damned*, she thought, *blackened and damned;* and stumbling over the rough clods beside Alec she studied him furtively until he turned and smiled down at her, a wavering smile that made his mouth seem suddenly weak. She bent her eyes to the ground again, ashamed of him and of herself, choking back the frantic thought of Margaret and pushing away with numb defensive caution any visions of the future.

With Alec snatching at dried sunflower heads and rasping out with his thumb the sharp brittle seeds, they walked across the field and through

the fence toward the lower lot. Past the barn
they could see Margaret raking and burning
leaves in the yard, and the fragrant smoke of
the fires lay upon the still air like incense.

Elspeth tightened her grasp on Alec's arm.

"Alec, I'm afraid!"

They stopped briefly, and Alec's thumb
rubbed at the bare seed-head while he looked
at her.

"Go in alone," he said. "She's seen us, so
don't try to slip in the back. Everything will be
all right."

"I can't face her," Elspeth whispered.

"You can," said Alec, "and you will. Go on,
now. I'll stop at the barn."

She was led along, desperately afraid of that
walk she must make alone past Margaret and
into the house, smothering as unworthy and
wild the half-formed wish that Alec would lead
her boldly up to the house, speak his love for
her, and carry her away. She clung to him
tightly in the shelter of the barn, and then he
was pulling her arms away and talking to her to
give her courage.

At last, armored with a tight shell of composure, she stepped out around the barn, across the lawn past Margaret.

"Back again," Margaret said. "Lovely day for a walk, isn't it?"

"Yes," Elspeth said. "A lovely day."

She smiled at her sister with stiff lips, and went on into the house.

Alec, watching Elspeth closely during the following days, soberly following her with his eyes, aware of the mischief he might have done, was surprised to find that after the first terror the girl seemed happy and even gay. She sang about the house, and at night when they played whist or sat reading, her words had a wit and a natural bantering edge that even he could find no hysteria in. Her eyes were full of laughter when she looked at him generally, but on three or four occasions they widened luminously and her mouth smiled, and when at these times she let down the shield of make-believe he knew that she had accepted him as lover, had tossed her watchfulness and her qualms and her affection for Margaret to the reckless winds.

Before a week had passed the two met in the barn after Ahlquist and the Grimmitsch boys had finished milking, and clung and kissed in the dim, beast-smelling twilight, and climbed together into the loft. Frequently in the evening Elspeth went down with Alec to watch the milking, and there, hidden from the other men by the high sides of the stall, she could lean against the manger and watch his hands and hear the soft hiss of milk into foam, and he could turn his face away from the cow's flank and purse his lips for a kiss, and get it, and they could talk trivial nonsense for the others, but only they two could read the real meaning of their words.

Those evenings were often exciting and gay and thoughtless, but over them was the shadow of discovery, and in Elspeth, despite the excitement of passion, a sneaking sense of shame and guilt and regret. Wholehearted as her love was, and fanned by secrecy and broken taboos, there were many times when she could think of herself and Alec as nothing but criminal and vicious, and many of their trysts in the loft were begun or ended in shameful tears.

One evening Alec had sent the Grimmitsch brothers to his east farm for chicken feed. He and Ahlquist were milking, and Elspeth leaned against the manger in the closed stall. The shame was upon her, and with the ring of the pail in her ears she stood fixed in a sad catalepsis, wide-eyed staring, the gloom of the darkening barn a gelid medium supporting the shadowy thrust of stalls in a long row like the piers of ruined bridges jutting into a river of liquefied dark.

She heard Ahlquist's grunt as he finished his last cow, the clatter of metal as he emptied his bucket into the tall milk can, and his heavy footsteps retreating as he went up to the men's house to wash for supper.

Then the girl's voice came out of the trance that held her, and she heard it like no voice, like something frail and brittle that rode the quiet dark as milkweed pods ride a stream.

"We're so horribly lost, Alec!"

The quality of her voice, the strange far-off wail of anguish under its quietness, brought a startled "Eh?" from Alec, and the whish of milk ceased.

"We're lost. We love each other without right and we stab Margaret without reason. I rob her of you, you rob her of me, we leave her nothing, and we have nothing ourselves but our love, and that's unclean."

The words hung and passed, as if someone upstream had stopped dropping pods on the water. Through the dark barn rose the murmur of obscure life, a stamp or the swish of a tail, the low munch of ruminating cows.

"What do ye want to do?" Alec asked quietly.

"I'm selfish," Elspeth said bitterly. The trance had passed, and her words stung.

"I'm selfish! I want you, and I don't want to hurt Margaret. Oh, Alec!"

Neither of them had heard the steps approaching from the house, neither of them had seen Margaret's figure darken the opaque square of the door. Tight now in each other's arms, Elspeth stammering and passionately clinging, her words a jargon of passion and desire, they neither saw nor heard the woman who stood stricken and unbreathing in the shadow.

When the flame in their blood was hot, Alec drew her to the ladder leading up into the loft, and she climbed willingly. Then they heard the gasp the shadow gave, the stumble of her feet on the sill, and against the almost-dark of the door they saw her running.

Elspeth's hands clawed at the rungs of the ladder, her legs went numb and she half-fell into Alec's arms.

"Almighty God!" Alec said.

He held Elspeth tightly, but she slid free and sank on the floor, and her grief came out of her in a long shuddering moan. In the dark a cow moved against the forgotten pail, and the clatter of tumbling tin was like an explosion in the hollow barn.

Alec made no move to recover it, but stood silently above the vague huddle of Elspeth's dress, while the shadowy interior heaved around them with its murmurous swell of beast-sounds.

At last he stooped and lifted the girl to her feet, and his voice was like the voice of one dying in bed after a long illness.

"We'd best go in and face it now," he said.

4

WHEN MARGARET TURNED and ran stumbling from the barn there was no room for thoughts in her mind. She never knew how she got into the house and up to her room. Numb with black bewildered grief, she sat on the edge of the bed, and gasping for air, ripped loose her high collar with icy shaking hands, convulsed alternately by tears and blasts of hot fury that shook her till she chattered.

The front door opened below, and her body froze erect as she listened. She heard no voices, but she knew they were whispering, wondering where she was, and she could see them in imagination standing like conspirators at the foot of the stairs. Her teeth clicked at the thought that they might be plotting to go away together.

Then there was the bell for the men, and Minnie's strident voice calling supper, and in a moment Alec's answer.

"Oh, aye," she heard him say. "Put ours away for a while, Minnie. We won't be eating just yet."

Margaret's teeth clicked again in furious indignation that he could still speak, still answer a call to dinner, still control the commonplace trivialities of that other life that had been theirs.

She heard no more words, though her breath was held with listening, only a low mutter of Alec's voice to which Elspeth apparently did not answer, and Elspeth's dragging footsteps on the stairs. The steps hesitated at the top, and the listener heard the short jerky breath of sobs before the sounds went down the hall and were lost behind the shutting of Elspeth's door. Almost at the same instant the front door slammed below.

Even then it was clear to Margaret that there was no triumph in the two, but that revelation brought her no comfort. Their misery was the reward for deadly sin; hers was undeserved, unearned, unbearable!

"My *sister!*"

She spat the words hissing into the dark, sitting straight on the bed adding the favors and the kindnesses she had done Elspeth, thinking of Alec and his periodic drinking, transforming subtly her mad jealousy into puritan censure, shifting the burden of furious personal affront to the religion she had been bred in, sublimating her own wrong into deadly sin against the Calvinist God, until she could approach a sad resignation to her lot and to the sinfulness of her relatives. Margaret had lost her husband and her sister; that was undeserved and bitter, but she could bear it. But Alec and Elspeth had lost their immortal souls, and a lifetime of expiation could never make their peace with a stern God.

By slow degrees Margaret's jealousy was transformed and masked, but the progress toward resignation was broken by paroxysms of rebellious fury, and the image that filled her mind was not of the lost souls before the tribunal of a just God, but of two shadows fumbling for the ladder to the loft.

For hours that image kept leaping out of the dark to scald her with hot resentment and burn away in an instant the laborious rationalizations of an hour. In the midst of one of these fits she leaped from the bed, lighted the lamp, and with

fingers that trembled clumsily in their haste,
stripped off her clothes to the last shred. Then
she stood before the mirror studying her naked
body—she who had never allowed Alec to
watch her undress, who had almost turned her
eyes from her own nakedness, now stood peering, lifting the lamp and turning half sidewise
to study herself in profile, running an experi-
mental hand down the smooth flank to the
swelling of a hip, stiffening her shoulders to cor-
rect the almost imperceptible sag of her breasts.

The mirror was high, and so she climbed
upon the bed to see herself full length, stren-
uously ignoring the high flush on the face in the
mirror, staring at the slim legs, the white wom-
anly body, thinking "Unwanted wife, unwanted
wife, unwanted wife." Her eyes lifted to meet
the eyes of the woman in the mirror, she
stepped off the bed to stare closely into them,
and then with a strong shudder she blew out
the lamp and threw herself on the bed where
she lay stiff with shame at herself, and the tears
came on again.

Through the long sleepless night she lay re-
volving the bitter cycle from passionate protest

to puritan judgment, fumbling for a way out, for a pattern of action, trying to imagine what the others would do, furiously crying that it didn't matter what they did, she could never forgive them. Alec could never again be her husband, Elspeth was irrevocably her sister no longer. Even if she could live on in the same house with them, and even if they wanted that, even if she could continue the patterns of decent and regular life, nothing would ever again be the same, and she could never forgive them. Neither her jealousy nor her religion would allow that.

At the end of the hall Elspeth too lay sleepless in grief as strong as Margaret's own. Several times she half-rose from the bed, intending to go to Margaret on her knees, but always the image of herself knocking timidly on a stern unopened door prevented her. There would be no forgiveness behind that door—there shouldn't be. She had no right. There was nothing she could beg for except her sister's pity, and pity would not help what was done. Nothing could help any of them, nothing, nothing. She tried to pray, and shrank from the unclean thing she was.

At two ends of the hall lay two women—the one bitter, hurt, justifying her jealousy in Calvinistic sternness and then tearing off the veil to expose herself as a scorned and insulted woman, the other lacerated by a guilt that admitted no extenuation, a guilt whose enormity was now increased tenfold by the shame of discovery. Both were listening unconsciously for Alec's step below, both caught up by the emotional ionization of the charged air in that dark corridor, whereby all shame and guilt clustered at the door of the miserable girl, all accusation and jealous wrath at the door of the wronged wife. Both were listening for Alec's step on the stair, not because either wanted him to come to her, not because either during that night had any room for love of him, but for a reason that neither could have expressed and that neither would have recognized—that without him their conflict did not exist.

Margaret, naked in the big walnut bed, lay wondering if he would try to come to her, if he

would dare; lay wondering what she would do
if he did, not wanting him but listening for the
sound of his heavy shoes. There was nothing to
discuss, she told herself. Everything that
needed saying they had said in the barn. Yet
when Alec did not come, and the secret boards
in walls and floor creaked with the passing of
interminable hours, and the light grayed the
windows to translucent squares, she was conscious of a dull disappointment, as if his coming
might have made some magic that would
change this dismal nightmare back into reality,
as if she had lain waiting all night to be released
from this fear and had found that it was no bad
dream to be brushed aside with a word of in-
cantation. And as she rose to dress the puritan
stiffness in her hardened and tightened, and the
face that she wore when she went downstairs
was gray, expressionless, calm as stone.

Alec spent the night in the barn, pacing up
and down the soft beast-smelling corridor between the rows of stalls, puttering at mending
a broken tug, climbing to the loft to throw down

more hay into the mangers, going on impulse
into the box stall where Elspeth's two calves lay
and scratching their hard polls. His thoughts
drove him to activity, and he lighted the lantern
to spend an hour cleaning stalls and pitching
manure out the square hole at the end of the
barn. He went out into the chilly dark and
sacked corn to be carried to the hogs in the
morning. In a frenzy of industry he did all the
odd jobs he could find, and when those ran out
he sat down on the bench in the harness room
with the lantern swinging slightly in the draft
from a broken pane, and filed all the saws he
owned, fiercely pleased with the screech of
steel on steel, soothing raw nerves with a noise
that he would have ordinarily found unbearable
after five minutes.

If he wondered at all about how he and Elspeth would face Margaret in the morning he
shouldered his way through the thought and left
it behind. In his mind, as in Elspeth's, their
guilt was plain and unpardonable. In that brief
moment when they were halted at the foot of
the ladder by Margaret's gasp and the stumbling of her feet, he had been tied away from
Elspeth as if by chains, and linked indissolubly

to Margaret by his own realization of her wrong. What happened to them now was in Margaret's hands.

Morning found him huddled in a horseblanket, shivering in the draft from the broken window. He had apparently been asleep, although he remembered nothing about finishing the saws. With the precision of long habit he went to the men's quarters, took the milk pails from their hooks, roused Ahlquist and the Grimmitsch brothers, and went out to the milking. Following that he soused his head in the icy water of the windmill trough, washed his hands carefully, and walked back to the house, calling to Ahlquist to feed the hogs.

As he opened the front door Elspeth was coming downstairs. They stood facing each other for a moment, Elspeth pale and nervous, Alec standing stupidly anguished with his mouth half-open and his red wet hair on end, before the girl came down and passed him going into the dining room. In that moment were said all their farewells, as in that other moment last night in the barn their passion had been cut suddenly, as a nerve is cut.

Alec followed her into the dining room, intent

on bearing his part in the self-immolation she had apparently decided upon.

But there was no immolation. Margaret, setting the breakfast table, met them with a cold "Good morning" and went on with her work. She was composed, but her greeting had an edge that cut. It drove Elspeth to a pathetic helpfulness that fussed with dishes and cream and sugar and was miserably clumsy. Alec silently sat down to his oatmeal and bacon and eggs. After his eighteen-hour fast and the all-night furious working he was ravenous, and Margaret, bending stolidly to her food, let a twinge of jealous pique show through her stone mask at the sight of his wolfish appetite. She herself ate very little, and Elspeth even less.

Alec rose before his last mouthful was swallowed, and started out.

"Got to get to work," he mumbled.

Elspeth too sprang up to carry their plates into the kitchen, still driven by the need to show her contrition in helpfulness.

To Margaret, as to the others, that first meeting had been stiff, wintry, inhumanly cold. She was thankful that at least it had been free from accusation or appeals for forgiveness, but as she sat quietly finishing her breakfast she looked across the table into the comfortless future, and the sternness of her unforgiving was bleak in her eyes.

They passed the last week of October, and November wore through dismal repetitive days, and December came on. Two or three times Alec took Ahlquist and drove into Sac City or Spring Mill or Wall Lake, and the two women did not see him for forty-eight hours. On those days Margaret would be grimmer than usual, and Elspeth, creeping timidly about the house with dustpan and broom, would see her sitting motionless in the hard mahogany rocker in the darkened parlor, stiff, unmoving, her face showing bonily and her eyes cavernous in the wintry gloom, no ray or gleam of light about her or about the room, not even enough to show on the decorative gold band of the picture molding or on the brooch at her throat. Elspeth knew she was not waiting for Alec, for the blind was tight down on the window that commanded the

road from town. Yet she was: she was waiting
with every nerve strained, with a seethe of con-
tradictory emotions under the masklike face.
She was waiting for Alec with some need to
know that he had been drinking again, some
positive necessity to find him guilty of more and
more and yet more crimes against her and God.
In his further damnation was the justification of
her vindictiveness; and she sat for hours together in the chilly parlor with the blinds drawn
against the sunless light of outdoors, waiting
and waiting and waiting for the crunch of
wheels in the gravel and the sounds of Ahlquist
half-carrying him off to the stable to sober up.

Yet she was kind, with a malignant kindness
that martyred itself with every gesture of sis-
terly or wifely solicitude. To Elspeth, mourn-
fully watching the transfiguration of all three of
them, her sister's natural impulses to love
seemed all to have soured into cold courtesy
and unfailing calculated tact. When company
called, as it frequently did after snow fouled the
roads and stopped any but inside work, she always sent Minnie to bring Alec in from crib or
barn; sat composed and charming, drawing her
husband and Elspeth into the conversation, lis-

tened smiling to their talk; maintained her perfect composure and her old aristocratic dignity. And Alec still, in company, called her "my lady" in a ritual of respect, and Elspeth fought back the strangling desire to cry, learned to smile and nod and inquire about commonplaces. And always behind the united family front was the intangible shadow of estrangement, an atmosphere of loveless frigidity nurtured by wrong and fattened by the silence that seemed to the three to have soaked into the very walls of the house, to have become a haunting presence that shouted soundlessly through the footsteps on the stairs or echoed in the slamming of a door.

They never spoke of the false front they offered to friends and neighbors, never planned it, never agreed upon it. It was simply there, a part of Margaret's implicit insistence on decency and decorum, a part on their side of a hopeless and endless expiation.

One morning Margaret told Ahlquist to hitch up the team, packed a bag, and came down in traveling dress to fling a dare in the face of the two.

"I'm going to Chicago to do my Christmas

shopping," she said. "I'll be gone about four days."

Coolly overlooking the fact that in going she left together the two who had betrayed her before, ignoring their situation with an audacity that made Elspeth gasp, she climbed into the buggy.

"I'll have Henning meet you at the station," Alec said.

During the time they were alone Elspeth saw Alec for hardly fifteen minutes altogether. He ate with the men and seldom came into the house during the day, and she was grateful. There was no reason why she should seize the opportunity to tell him. It would come out soon enough. The certainty of that sent her feverishly to her room every day to work over clothes that would conceal her longer, hide this nightmare within nightmare close in the secret darkness of her womb, this feeding parasite that wasted her body and desolated her mind, this child of sin that at almost every meal her body tried to repudiate in nausea. Her strained efforts to eat naturally, her eyes that she knew were sunken and terrified, her face drained of blood in the struggle to keep down her sickness, could not escape Margaret for long, and even if it did there would soon be the shape of her to betray her.

It would come out soon enough; there was no need to tell Alec. There was not even any desire to talk to Alec, any feeling for him as the father of the nightmare. That passion had smothered in the airless prison of guilt.

When Margaret came back and Alec stood by the wheel to help her down, Elspeth was on the steps, her hands clasped in front of her partly from timidity but more from the fear that her shape had already begun to betray her. After four days she half-hoped for a smile, for a greeting with a hint of warmth in it, but she saw Margaret take Alec's helping hand as if it were the hand of a groom, and she shrank back to make way as her sister swept up the walk and into the house with a curt nod. Because her eyes were lowered Elspeth did not see the sharp look that Margaret gave them both, the prying glance that searched for guilt even be-

yond their first immeasurable guilt, and thought
it found what it searched for. But Elspeth did
not see that look; she only smelled the clean
new smell of Margaret's clothes, sensed the air
of comfortable opulence in the fur neckpiece
and the smart traveling suit, felt only the sick-
ening inferiority of her own plain dress, her own
appearance, her own qualities of mind and body
and soul, to the high excellence that inhered in
everything Margaret's.

She went meekly into the house and helped
Minnie prepare dinner while Margaret sat upstairs surrounded by the unopened bags and
parcels that Alex had brought in, biting her lips
with vexation at her foolishness in leaving the
two alone. Their very humility gave them away.
She had been a fool, a fool, fool, fool! During
the ride out from town she had been almost
passionately anxious to see them, to find them
innocent and smiling again, but the lugubrious
timidity of Elspeth in the doorway twisting
her hands in her apron and Alec's frozen stiffness as he helped her down had been too full
of the consciousness of guilt. She knew in her
heart that they had sinned again, and once

more the unforgiving core in her hardened.

Yet she was kind; in spite of herself, in defiance of herself, in defiance of her religion and her jealousy, there would creep out in her words and actions a feeling for their comfort. When, on Christmas Eve, she held the party that had been traditional with them for years, and invited the tenant farmers and their families to the house for games and refreshments and gifts, she made with her own hands, almost lovingly, the haggis that Alec loved, and she swallowed her repugnance for drink to send Ahlquist into Spring Mill for Christmas ale and wine. But when the tenants were gone and she could not find Alec she knew that Ahlquist had brought more than ale and wine, and that if she wanted to look she would find the two in the harness room with a bottle of whisky.

In a scorching fury she waited in the parlor until Elspeth had gone forlornly to bed, waited until the house was quiet and the four candles in the dining room threw wavering shadows in the deserted hall. Then she went to her room, carried downstairs the gifts she had bought in

Chicago, and arranged them carefully under the Christmas tree; with furious care she placed them so that the name cards were up. "Christmas greetings to Elspeth from Margaret." "The Seasons Best Wishes to Her Husband from His Loving Wife: Alec from Margaret." Tinseled and gilded paper with snow scenes upon it, and her own careful printing underneath. Above them, when she had finished, she stood with clenched hands,—too bitter to smile at the irony of her giving,—and then she blew out the candles and went up to the bedroom whose door had never been open to Alec since that night in October, whose door he had never since tried to enter.

When the house was quiet again and the only sound was the rasp of bare oak limbs against the shingles, Elspeth quietly opened her door, tiptoed breathlessly past her sister's room down the stairs to the Christmas tree, and there laid beside the packages of Margaret her own offering, presents for both Alec and Margaret, things she had ordered by letter from Sac City the last time Ahlquist had been in.

And Elspeth had barely crept as soundlessly as a mouse back to her room before Alec opened the front door, creaked drunkenly to the tree, and laid his gifts beside the others in the dark.

None of them ever forgot the mockery of that Christmas, that gift-giving; that intolerable dinner whose turkey and dressing and cranberry sauce and delicate sweet ham and heaped vegetables and pumpkin and mince pie and papery-thin oatcake fairly shrieked for someone to enjoy it; that groaning table about which the three of them sat crushed by the heavy silence of the house, grateful for Minnie's clatter in the kitchen, grim with the cold thanks and the joyless unwrapping of presents, mocked by the Christmas tree glinting with decorations in the hall. None of them ever forgot how the kingly food was ashes in the mouth, how the gifts were bitter hostages to the hollow life they had tacitly consented to lead, derisive burlesques of affection and friendliness. And none of them, sitting without appetite at table, dressed for the holiday, stiff in broadcloth and brocade, could see any hope or promise in a future that stretched through interminable years frozen by the same unforgiveness and threaded always by the same guilt and shame.

Now December was done and over, and the snow of January piled in heavy curling drifts over fences and coops and against the windward faces of house and barn, and toward the end of January Margaret knew what she had suspected for some time. Elspeth had felt her eyes before; on a day when the snow was falling outside in coin-broad flakes, when the stair door was closed to keep the heat from going upstairs and the heatless parlor was shut tight, the girl sat in the dining room by the window when Margaret entered and stood in the doorway watching her. There were no words. Even Elspeth's impulse to shrink and cry out was never translated into action. Her head did not turn after the first sidelong look; her eyes remained fixed on the quiet flakes outside the window. And Margaret, intently staring, satisfied herself that what she believed was true, and left the room.

Then there were two of them sitting by the windows watching the feathery fall of snow: Elspeth by the boxed geraniums in the dining room, Margaret on the hard mahogany rocker in

the icy parlor, both outwardly calm, both lacerated inwardly by emotions made all the
stronger by their repression.

Margaret sat in the cold for over an hour, not
heeding the periodic tense shivers that ran
through her limbs, or the slow retreat of blood
from hands and feet, or the tightening of throat
and jaw in the chilly air. At last she rose quietly,
threw a walking cape over her shoulders, and
went outside. Elspeth saw her hurrying through
the thick flakes to the men's house, saw her
knock and stand waiting, her bare head powdered with white, saw Ahlquist come to the
door and motion her in, saw the shake of her
head. Then after a moment Ahlquist came out
in a mackinaw and the two went across the lot
and disappeared in the stable.

The girl felt no curiosity about what she
saw. Margaret knew now—what she would do
about it was locked behind the inscrutable
stone mask she wore. Whatever she did it
could not be worse than this endless and hopeless contrition, this purgatory of despairing
expiation.

If Margaret could see it, others would soon

be able to, but that thought was only a dull unhappiness, a moping wonder that she, Elspeth MacLeod, should be with child, and at the mercy of the sort of people who galloped about the countryside with such news. The tears that came were not tears of anguish, but of defenseless despairing shame; she sat with her knees touching the window box full of winter blooms, and watched the still, hurrying snow build hooded covers for every branch and twig in the oak outside, watched the brown clotted earth left by a recent thaw disappear slowly under the white.

On my grave, she thought, *quiet snow on a quiet grave; yes, I do wish it, and the ache gone and the fever and only the cool and the snow. Maybe I'll die with the child, and end it for all of us, and there'll be no more forgetting, no more trying not to remember.*

She thought of her quiet life in Glasgow, of her childhood and her mother, and the songs her mother had sung about the house. One particularly, an old ballad, and with the impact of a thrown missile the pertinence of that ballad to her own life struck her.

Word's gane to the kitchen,
And word's gane to the ha,
That Marie Hamilton gangs wi' bairn
To the hichest Stewart of a'.

Even the name, she thought; even the
Stuart, and Margaret the auld Queen. The
memory of her mother's figure dusting about
the house was sharp reality, and the falling
strains of the last stanza with its laconic implications of tragedy brought the tears so thick that
she couldn't see the geraniums or the wavering
snow.

Over and over, whispering, she sang the last
stanza:—

Last nicht there was four Maries,
The nicht there'l be but three;
There was Marie Seton, and Marie Beton,
And Marie Carmichael, and me.

"And me," she said, and caught her tears in
her hands.

———

Out in the barn Margaret faced Ahlquist's un-hurried questioning, her face drawn with cold and her eyes fixed on his impassive face. Ahl-quist did not speak; he merely stood and waited as he seemed to wait for everything: fatalistic and immobile, like a great sad-eyed dog.

"You still want to go back to Norway?" Margaret asked. The strain she was under gave her words a harsh, snarling quality.

The Viking nodded and waited, patient, apparently not even curious.

"No matter what they say of you, or why they think you went?"

"What will that matter?" said Ahlquist simply. "I won't be here."

He knows! Margaret thought. He knows why I brought him out here and what I'm going to ask.

"I'll give you two hundred dollars to go back to your country," she said swiftly. "On one condition. Two, rather. Do you agree?"

In the Viking's eyes she caught something very like sympathy, and behind that a veiled irony, a quick intuitive intelligence that waited for her to come to the point he had already guessed.

[114]

"I never talk," Ahlquist said. "And I want to go right away. Is that it?"

"To-night," Margaret said. "And you leave secretly. You tell no one you're going."

She pulled her purse from under the cape and opened it. As she began to count out bills the Norwegian interrupted her.

"One hundred is enough," he said. "I'd do it for you and Miss MacLeod for nothing if I had enough of my own to get me there."

Margaret's imperious control of herself gave way like an uncoiling spring. Her hand shook as she wadded an uncounted bundle of money into his hand and turned hastily to the door. Her "Thank you, Ahlquist," was choked and almost inaudible. After the door swung shut behind her Ahlquist stood quietly, his lips puckered and his face like that of a melancholy friendly big dog, and then he shoved the bills in his pocket and went back to his quarters to pack. Sometime before night, in the thick shrouding snowfall, he disappeared.

After dinner, when Elspeth had gone to her room and Alec sat reading the county newspaper, Margaret entered the dining room and spoke to him, her words tight, clipped, coldly restrained, but with something in her tone that hinted hysteria, as if that calm voice could at any moment break into cracked screaming.

"Ahlquist's gone," she said.

Alec lowered his newspaper. "Yes. How did you know?"

"I sent him."

"You what?"

"I gave him the money and asked him to go."

The hard tight vertical line appeared between Alec's brows and he dropped the paper on the floor. His voice, when it came, was flat.

"Why?"

Margaret—facing him squarely, seeing the anger in his eyes, feeling her own control going, fighting for it, hearing the hysteric edge in her words, wanting to blast him with her fury and hurt, and fighting that because she wanted to tell him calmly and cruelly—ended the deadlock of eyes and wills by spitting the words in his face.

"Because Elspeth's going to have a baby. You hear? My sister's going to have a baby!"

Her voice escaped her entirely, rose to a furious scream. "You hear? You hear? Now do you know why I gave him the money and sent him away? He knows. He knew already, and he knows the story we'll allow people to spread around. He knows he'll father a child not his. *But other people won't know!* You see now? You see why I sent him away?"

She caught at breath and control, and the frenzied scream died to a tense monotone.

"You left me no other choice. There's no one would marry her this far along, and there were only two men people could pin it on."

The anger in Alec's eyes had been replaced by something stubborn and defensive.

"I'll no try to deny the child, Margaret."

"But you will!" said Margaret. "You've left me little enough, but that little I'll keep. If I have to I'll tell it myself, on my own sister, that Ahlquist is the man. You've taken what really counted, but I'll keep the husk of it, the name of it. You hear?"

And Alec, seeing her with the mask off, feeling the depth of her hurt, nodded slowly, knowing that whatever she demanded of him in future he would agree to.

"So be it then," he said.

5

ELSPETH'S CHILD WAS BORN in June, a year almost to the day after she had arrived from Scotland. For three weeks the girl lay in her bed with her sunken bright eyes fixed on Margaret as she came and went with food, with changes and wrappers for the infant, with books and fruit and embroidery—books Elspeth never read, fruit she never ate, embroidery that never occupied her fingers. They piled up on the stand by her elbow while she watched Margaret with stricken eyes, and after a day or two Margaret would take them away and bring others. Always the older sister compelled speech into the narrow channel of the necessary, brief greetings and "good nights," inquiries as to the patient's comfort, suggestions of foods.

For she was kind. Even the armor of her efficiency could not hide that. Elspeth and the child were waited on by no one else. She would hardly even let Minnie prepare the broths and custards that went in to the sick woman. But when Elspeth nursed the baby Margaret would stand watching for a moment—for just a moment—with something lost and hungry on her lips and in her eyes, and then she would turn and go out.

And Elspeth would think of Margaret's letters in the past, of how she had wanted a child, of the time when she thought she was going to, and the disappointment showing in the quiet written words when she told her sister that she apparently never could now. *And now one in the house,* Elspeth thought; *and it not hers, so terribly not hers, and not mine either, not really mine.* And she would hug the forlorn sickly little waif to her in an agony of love that could never be love, that could only be fear and reproach and sorrow, that would never quite forgive the agony of its birth and its fatherlessness.

When Margaret spoke to her after she was well again about christening the child, Elspeth shrank, feeling her son a child of darkness, never to be taken brutally out into the light for a public ceremony, unworthy of the ministrations of even such a minister as the Reverend Hitchcock. She could see the reactions of people she knew, hear their tongues wag.

"Must he be . . . ?"

"Of course he must," said Margaret. "He has to have a name. Have you thought of one?"

Elspeth shook her head. Then, abruptly, as if offering her baby as an expiatory sacrifice, she said, "Would you give him a name?"

Margaret thought a moment, and when she spoke it was with unconscious cruelty.

"There's never been a Malcolm in our family. Would that do? Malcolm MacLeod?"

And Elspeth, thinking, "That's the way she puts it: *There's never been a Malcolm in our family*—as if he weren't worthy a name any of us have had," assented with a mute nod.

The next Sunday, through the silence and the veiled whispers of the few stragglers who had remained after church to watch, Margaret walked almost proudly up the aisle with the child squalling in her arms, and he was christened Malcolm MacLeod and dedicated to the service of Christ on earth. Elspeth was not there, nor was Alec.

And the years,—the stifling nights of summer, windless and humid, the hot oppressive blackness when the three lay awake in different rooms listening to the petulant discomfort of the child and the curtains hung slack in wide-open windows; the interminable days when clothes clung to perspiring bodies and the oaks drooped under the fierce sun and the darkened parlor was the only passably cool room in the house; the slow ripening of September, the golden fields, the farm alive with strange men, huskers and threshers powdered with the bright dust of harvest, and in full view from the window of the haymow the incredible streak of flame that was the creek bed; and in October also the still wavering fall of leaves,—and in the intervals between labor and labor the wild regret that was never to die, but was to be hidden in silence and unforgiving and the avoidance of outward feeling until over it grew a shell of habit, so that for days at a time the three forgot the reasons for their watchful silence and the bleakness of their house. . . .

Winter swept its drifts against the broad barn; and the chickens (Elspeth's quail among them, now completely forgotten), pecked their wheat gingerly out of the granular snow. Every morning while light still seemed only a ghostly reflection from the drifts there would be the sound of saws as the Grimmitsch brothers worked at the woodpile, and there would be shouts as they drove the cattle after milking out into the pen where they would stand quietly with their breath blooming like flowers about their heads.

And the long rains of spring—when fields and roads were impassable quagmires and the overflowing creek spread out into the flats where in summer sunflowers grew; and after a time the green thrust of tulip and crocus blades against the warm south wall of the house, the fat popping of lilac buds, the yellow burgeoning of leafless forsythia, and from the loft window a countryside misted with green as delicate as thin smoke . . .

And the slow timeless revolution of the seasons—while the boy Malcolm grew frailly, and walked, and then talked, and his age became successively two and three and four and five, and he could be taken out in the buggy by Uncle Alec, and the two sharp-featured women in the big house would watch with emotions that they had almost ceased to recognize, but with an inflexible tight-lipped taciturnity as ingrained as the habits of sleeping or eating . . .

More and more they began to look alike. Elspeth, who never went out, even to church, dressed in sober black as if in a kind of mourning, and after the child was born Margaret too lost gradually the delight in dress that had made her the style-setter of a county, that had led her into Chicago or Omaha two or three times a year, that had filled her attic with fashion magazines and patterns and trunks of discarded clothes. In public Alec no longer called her "my lady." Her hair was no longer carefully pompadoured, but combed straight back from her high bony forehead. Her dresses, like Elspeth's, were fusty black relieved only by a bit of lace at the collar and the gold locket watch at her breast. By slow transition her dignity hardened into a stiff-backed formality.

Yet still, rigidly clinging to the patterns of her

old life, she entertained neighbors and towns-
people, defying their gossip until the passing
years made it no longer a matter of any moment. Her table still groaned with food on
Christmas and Thanksgiving and Easter, and
though her parties lacked the gaiety that in old
times had echoed through the rooms, she kept
her friends. Even the children, who might have
been afraid of her rigid black-frocked figure,
were only curious. Something in her led them
to come up and stare into her face. Something
—perhaps her startling eyes, perhaps some
subtly communicated kindliness beneath the
forbidding old-maidishness of her person, made
them come to her as they never came to
Elspeth.

Alec, having given up the night Ahlquist left,
poured his energies into his farms. When Malcolm was five years old he bought two full sec-
tions of rich bottom land adjoining his east
acreage and recorded it in the boy's name.
Every autumn when the rents came in he made
a special trip to town to deposit them in Malcolm's account. At every opportunity he took
the boy with him to the fields, on drives, into

Chicago. When he was elected to the State Senate in Malcolm's sixth year they went together to Des Moines and stayed together through the entire session, Alec stuffing his nephew with candy, loading him with skates and sleds and toys, taking him to shows and plays. It was as if, single-handed, he was attempting to counteract the boy's home environment; as if by dragging him into the air, into the city, around the farms, he was trying to eradicate the pallor, blow away the timidity and silence that the child absorbed from the very walls of the house he lived in, relieve him from the psychic repression of the two women who were bringing him up.

The years that had smoothed Margaret's pompadour to a flat mousy wig—that had sunk her eyes and sharpened the straight ridge of her nose, that had transformed her queenly figure to a gaunt shape in sober black—the years that had driven Elspeth out of youth and into middle age before she passed twenty-five, and had made her a soft-stepping, quietly rustling, timid, pallid-faced housekeeper—had touched Alec more lightly. The face was more florid, with almost infinitesimal veins showing on nose and cheekbones. He was heavier, and his very size gave him a senatorial air of solidity and prosperous householdership. In the company of men he was still a great laugher, fond of horse-play and convivial company, and he was ad-mired almost to adulation by the county he dominated. But around the house, with Elspeth or Margaret or even Malcolm, he moved and spoke guardedly, observing the wordless taboos of their relationship. Often he sat with a news-paper or a book for hours, ostensibly reading but actually watching the two women. And they, looking up to find his eyes on them, shifted un-der the brooding intensity of his look, squirmed like sullen rebuked children.

Malcolm and Alec were so much together that one winter Margaret was visited and revis-ited by a curious dream in which Alec and the boy walked hand in hand down a long gloomy corridor, and she could see their hands clasped together and their bare feet as they searched the shadowy pavement of the hall. Their hands and their bare feet and the glimmering white wedge of the boy's face she could always see as if a light shone out of the flesh, but Alec's face was no face in any of the recurrences of the dream, only a whitish blur that moved in the stealthy dark beside the white hands and white face and white moving feet of the boy. Miles and miles the two walked, the corridor opening always new gulfs of shadow before them. Sometimes Margaret's sleeping eyes saw them at a distance, the phosphorescent flesh wavering like incandescent moths in the dark. Then they were close, the boy's dark eyes upturned to the blur of Alec's face, and the sinews and cords of their linked hands clear to her watching eyes.

Four times Margaret had this dream, and each time she awoke clammy and trembling. For some reason that she could not define, that vaguely glowing blur above Alec's ghostly shoulders terrified her. And she never dreamed that dream without seeing at least once the close-up of those clinging and tightly clasped hands.

In the house Alec was always grave with Malcolm, but they went out frequently. What they did when they were gone Margaret never knew, but there was always warm color in the boy's cheeks when they returned, and in his eyes a lurking sly laughter as if over a secret joke, a sidelong twinkling glance that hardly rippled the decorum of his indoor face, but that caught its echo several times an evening in Alec's eyes.

Margaret never knew, but Elspeth did. One afternoon when Malcolm was eight she was picking peas and beans in the garden plot when she heard them coming up from the cornfield that now reached all the way to the flood plain of the creek. She heard Malcolm laugh, not the hesitant embarrassed chuckle that was his only evidence of lightheartedness around his two aunts—not that, but a gay, exuberant, whooping peal of merriment with all his lungs behind it, so startling that she bent farther below the protecting strip of sweet corn that screened her.

"You just ought to see one sometime," she heard Alec say. "There never were such caterpillars before or since. I skinned that one and we used his hide for a rug for years. It covered the whole hall floor where those rag ones are now. Finally the moths got to him and we had to throw him away."

"How long was his fur?" The boy's voice, cu-

rious, half-jeering in good-humored disbelief,
still gurgling with laughter.

"Oh, up to your knees, I expect. And thick!
Just like a jungle. The cat used to hunt rabbits
in it. He had a pelt, I tell you. If you happened
to walk across it barefooted before you went to
bed you couldn't sleep all night, you were so
tickled. Just lie in bed and laugh till you
ached."

"How could a moth eat his fur if it was so
thick?"

The voices were growing fainter. Elspeth's
straining ears just caught part of Alec's reply.

"These were Sac County moths. Big as a buz-
zard. Their jaws are gimlets that'll bore a two-
inch hole . . ."

Standing in the garden behind the protecting
fringe of sweet corn, Elspeth could see them
walking hand in hand toward the house, and
with an intuition that shrank at its own sharp-
ness she predicted the exact moment when,
passing the chicken yard, Malcolm's hand
dropped from Alec's and the two figures moved
apart to become not companions any more but
just two people walking with each other.

That evening Malcolm looked up from his book and saw his Aunt Elspeth watching him with something dewy and eager in her bright sunken eyes, saw her prim lips trembling into softness, and he smiled his slow hesitant smile in return, rather surprised to find such an expression on the face of either of his aunts. Then the warmth went out of his aunt's eyes and her lips tightened again, and Malcolm had no way of knowing that she had been trying to come out of the shell that bound her, that she had been urging him to laughter, trying to tell him that she too had known laughter and a light heart. She too remembered angleworms so long that a hen worked ten hours to pull one from its hole. She remembered the spotted cow that fell in the quicksand and came out a giraffe. She remembered nonsense and joyous preposterous horseplay, and all the hunger of nine years had been in her face as she looked at Malcolm.

But Malcolm had no way of knowing, and he did not even suspect that when his Aunt Elspeth left the room a moment later she went up to her room to cry with a bitterness that racked her bony chest and left her exhausted, to cry as she had not cried in nine years, and to lie miserably in the dark looking back through the loveless unforgiving repression that had become her life, remembering as she had never dared remember the few gay months after her arrival from Scotland when she was still a girl and laughter had not yet gone from her life.

And Alec had not forgotten. Away from the house he was teaching Malcolm to laugh, blowing out of him the rheumatic chilly damp of the bleak house, drawing him away from the depressing and frozen-faced kindness of his aunts. His aunts! Elspeth sneered in the face of that lie and what had come of it. Witches, the two of them, hags; one afraid to play with the boy because that would be presuming to show herself his mother, the other refusing because by doing so she condoned the crime of his birth, condoned her own betrayal by stooping to show affection for her sister's and her husband's son.

Hags, Elspeth thought, *witches that haunt the child and he growing up crushed and timid and pale, yet all of us loving him as we can love nothing else. Margaret too, I know she does, it shows in her, but she won't let herself admit it. All of us, and only Alec*

*able to help him at all, only Alec remembering laugh-
ter and a light heart.*

The years passed like sand under the feet of
the four, the seasons swung in the same long
rhythm from the first robin and the swelling lilac buds to breathless summer heat and the me-
tallic trill of locusts and in the evenings fireflies
starring the tangible velvet of the air; from the
dying flame of sumac and soft maple into the
long pointless waiting of winter, and back to
the thrust of crocus blades under the last snow.

The house grew old with its occupants, the
horsehair sofa was replaced by a broad oak settee with leather cushions, wallpaper changed at
three-year intervals, Wilton rugs covered the
floors instead of the worn Brussels carpets, but
actually there was little change from the somber
coloring of the years, no alleviation of the bleakness that was like a chill in the bones of the
building. Its rooms kept their imperviousness to
redecoration and warmth; laughter was as un-
thinkable as a bright dress on one of the sisters.

Nothing, not even the sisters, changed. They

might have been twins, and they might have been any age from thirty to fifty. In the two years after Malcolm's birth they had attained a kind of dry agelessness as durable as stone. Only their eyes remained youthful and alive, deeply sunken and ice-blue, bright, alert as the eyes of animals.

Nothing changed. Even Minnie, who had left them to be married to a farmer ten miles away, had seen her husband and her one child die in a flaming barn, and was back in her old place after a four-year absence.

Malcolm was with them only during the summers now. At fourteen he was sent to school in Sac City, where he boarded with friends. When he left, his two aunts silently packed his trunk and stood by the door watching, not waving, not even smiling, yet somehow communicating love, good wishes, solicitude. Having learned observation from his elders the boy had a feeling, as the last bundle was stowed away and as he sat waiting in the front seat of the Case automobile his uncle had bought that spring, that both women were very close to tears. A word or a gesture, he thought, might bring them to him

to shower him with kisses and hugs. But he
shrank from that possibility as he would have
shrunk from cursing them. The thought of either of them displaying any feeling was intolerable.

Alec swung the crank, the motor thundered,
and they were off down the lane of perfect
elms. When he looked back to wave, Malcolm
saw the two black figures still motionless against
the white wall of the house, and his wave received no answer.

For three years Malcolm left in this way,
wondering at the strangeness of his aunts, but
forgetting them in the warmth of his uncle's
company before they had passed Paxleys'. For
three years he returned in June to find the two
women standing just where he had left them
the autumn before, as if time had fixed them
forever in that attitude of silent hail and fare-
well. They greeted him with a word and a shake
of the hand and something in the eyes like a
smile, and there was nothing in their demeanor
to tell him that since early morning neither had
left her chair by a strategic window, and that
what he took for a softening like a smile in the

ice-blue eyes might have been caused by the strain of watching the road for hours as intently as one watches at a deathbed.

A few days after returning from his third year of high school Malcolm gave evidence that the long lie about his parentage was beginning to wear thin. Alec was tinkering with the car in the machine shed when the boy entered.

"Want a job?" Alec asked.

"Sure."

"Hold this."

Malcolm held the wrench while Alec fumbled underneath to tighten a nut, and as they leaned together over the motor the boy asked the question that had been burning in him for months.

"Look," he said. "Who am I?"

"Eh?"

Alec dropped the nut and groped for it an unnecessarily long time. When he raised his head whatever had been in his face was carefully veiled.

"Who am I?"

"My nephew. Who did you think you were, the Crown Prince?"

But Alec's jocularity left Malcolm untouched.

"No, I want to know who I really am. You say my mother was Aunt Margaret's sister who died, and that my father's dead too."

"That's right," Alec said quietly.

"Well," said Malcolm, "I met Jim Paxley in Sac City and he said 'Hello, Ahlquist.' Where'd he get that? Is my name really Ahlquist?"

"No," said Alec. "Take my word for it, your name's not Ahlquist."

"Seems to me I've heard that name before," Malcolm said. "Haven't I heard you mention somebody named Ahlquist that used to work for you?"

"Maybe. He went back to Norway before you were born."

"Well, why is my name MacLeod, when that's Aunt Elspeth's name, and Aunt Margaret's maiden name?"

"Accident," Alec said shortly. "Your mother happened to marry a man with the same name. There's plenty of MacLeods in Scotland. Whole clans of 'em."

"Maybe I'm just stupid," Malcolm said. "Paxley seemed to think it was a great joke to call me Ahlquist."

"It wouldn't take much to amuse that Paxley," Alec said. "Here, take the crank and turn it over slow, will you, while I have a look?"

During that summer Malcolm asked no more questions, but Alec was increasingly aware that the two women of the house were not the only ones who could hide their thoughts behind an impenetrable mask, and one night when they were alone he spoke to Margaret.

"We'll send Malcolm to Chicago to school the coming year."

"Why?"

"They're starting to call him Ahlquist in Sac."

The mask of Margaret's face did not change expression.

"In that case he'd better go to Chicago," she said.

Malcolm's departure for Chicago was delayed almost a month by an epidemic that closed the schools, so that it was early October before he

packed and got through the preliminaries of
leaving. Two nights before he was to go, the
boy and his aunts were sitting down to dinner
when Alec entered the front door. Margaret, at
the kitchen end of the table, looked up to see
him standing slumped and nerveless in the hall,
with his hand on the knob behind him, and her
fingers tightened on the dish she was passing.

Now he's taken to coming drunk to dinner, she
thought. Her blood was racing with the old furious protest, but the mask of her face was expressionless, and her "Will you have some
asparagus, Malcolm?" was quiet and even.

As Alec came in and sat down only Malcolm
spoke, and his ineffectual greeting trailed off
into the electric silence. In the lamplight Alec's
face looked ghastly: the eyes ringed darkly and
the lips touched faintly with blue. *Getting to look
like a drunkard,* said Margaret's hissing mind,
and bringing it in here for the boy to see.

Without a word, in the uncomfortable silence
that hung over the table, Alec reached out for
the dish Elspeth passed, helped himself, and
started to put it down. Then, while the eyes of
Malcolm were bent in embarrassment on the

food he was eating, while Margaret was burning behind her mask with the old violence that would never down, while Elspeth was rigid with the terror that came upon her when the tension of unspoken and hoarded wrong was in the air,—while all three thought him drunk and reacted to that belief,—Alec died instantly.

The dish dropped to the table, his body fell forward across the corner of the board, tipping it, and as the two women sprang up, Alec slid sideways, pulling the tablecloth and dishes down upon himself, and Malcolm leaped with a strangling cry to his uncle's side.

Minnie, running in from the kitchen at the crash, saw Margaret and Elspeth standing stiffly, their masks off now, Margaret's hand against her mouth to stifle a scream, Elspeth whimpering through contorted lips, and before them the wrecked table and Malcolm bending over his uncle's body.

Malcolm's head turned.

"Help me," he said.

With Minnie helping he carried Alec to the broad leather settee in the parlor, the two aunts trailing like sleepwalkers behind. There, after a frenzied five minutes of feeling for pulse in the stiffening wrist, Malcolm turned abruptly and ran outside. The three women stood silently in the gloomy parlor, and the bleakness of the house seeped upon them as heavy as black fog.

In the stillness they heard the automobile burst into full roar, heard the clash of its gears and the reckless explosion of gravel as it whirled heavily into the lane. Like one walking in sleep Margaret moved to pull the blinds upon the already dark room, brought the lamp from the dining room and set it, turned low, upon the mantel—moved it because it shed too much light on Alec's dead face.

Across the noise of Minnie's crying the two sisters looked at each other, their eyes meeting frankly for the first time in eighteen years.

"Maybe I'd better fix his bed," Elspeth said weakly. "Malcolm must have gone for the doctor."

"I'll fix it!"

Margaret went up the stairs with firm steps, and Elspeth, alone with the body of Alec, stood watching him, wanting to smooth the twisted lips and straighten the rumpled hair, but not daring. When she realized how fully she did not dare she went into the dining room and wept.

EPILOGUE

THERE WERE NO MORE BUGGIES or cars turning into the lane now. With a last look at the quiet spread of level countryside Margaret Stuart rose awkwardly from the little mahogany rocker, and the noise from the other rooms rose with her. The scent of flowers was overpowering, a sticky, decaying sweetness of roses and lilies strong with the smell of death.

Composedly, quietly, Margaret walked into the hall and through the people who greeted her and made way, into the dining room where before the windows Alec's coffin lay on a scaffolding completely smothered in flowers.

The noise of conversation and the sympathetic sniffling of women fell off gradually and died to a waiting silence as Margaret stood by the coffin and took a last look at her husband. Elspeth, sitting behind and to one side, saw no change in the parchment of her sister's face, no

quivering of the lips, no relaxation of the inflexible rigidity of her body. Then Margaret
stepped back, nodded to the minister, and sat
down between Elspeth and Malcolm while the
Reverend Hitchcock wet his red lips and bent
his head over the casket.

"Let us pray," he said.

For three quarters of an hour he bleated
through a panegyric on Alec Stuart, whom he
had never liked, and women standing in the hall
wiped their eyes furtively and men coughed.
Margaret sat dry-eyed, conscious of Elspeth and
Malcolm beside her on the high dining room
chairs, sensing with emotionless clearness the
violence of the boy's grief and Elspeth's tense
self-control, realizing with an almost smiling
wonder that the Reverend Hitchcock was even
more stupid than Alec and Elspeth had thought
him, rebelling at the voice bleating "In my
Father's house are m-aaaa-ny m-aaaa-nsions"
while she recalled Alec's contemptuous doubt
if the preacher had any blood in him at all. Fool
to plan a big funeral, she thought. Fool to have
Hitchcock preach—the only person in the room
who didn't like Alec, who isn't genuinely sorry,

and he giving the sermon, lying with every word, doing God's office for the fee in it.

And when the long ride to the cemetery and back was over, and the minister had taken his fee and gone and the buggies and cars had one by one passed through the tunnel of elms to the road, it was with a feeling of tired relief that Margaret took off her plain black bonnet and helped Minnie clear the house of the remaining flowers.

Since Alec's death Malcolm had been gloomily silent, wrapped in profound morbid isolation. After the funeral he spent the afternoon pacing back and forth through the crisp leaves of the back lawn, and both his aunts noticed the haggard weariness in the youth's face, the tight vertical wrinkle between his eyes that was so much like Alec's expression when angry or intent.

The wrinkle was still there at breakfast the next morning, and when the three were finished Malcolm rose.

"Will you come into the living room?" he said. "I have to talk to you."

There was something so troubled and unhappy and miserably stubborn in the boy's eyes
that Elspeth sat down with the old freezing anticipation of an emotional crisis, shooting an
oblique glance at Margaret to see if she felt it
too, but finding her sister's mask as expressionless as ever.

For some time the boy sat uncomfortably
studying his hands, and when he spoke it was
with an effort that strained his voice to the
cracking point. What he said, turning full toward Elspeth where she sat with her hands
twisted in her apron, was "You're my mother,
aren't you?"

Elspeth's breath hissed in her throat. The
gaunt figure of Margaret never moved.

"And Uncle Alec was my father, wasn't
he?"

Neither of the sisters answered.

"I'm sorry," Malcolm said wretchedly. "I'm
awfully sorry; but I've thought so for a long
while, and now I've got to know."

He looked at Elspeth stubbornly, and she
broke under his look to bury her face in the
back of the settee.

"I'm sorry," Malcolm mumbled again. Then he broke out to Margaret: "Did Uncle . . . Did my father leave a will?"

"You're taken care of," Margaret said. Her voice was flat, dead, carefully void of expression. "Two farms are in your name, and there's something like a thousand dollars in your account in Sac City. There's also a thousand dollars in cash left you in his will, and five thousand in bonds for your schooling."

"So much?"

In the boy's words there was no exultation, only a sad wonder that death should have left him with what would have been under ordinary circumstances boundless wealth.

"I'm going away," he said. "I'll need some of that money—not all."

"I'll get your bank book."

Margaret went quietly out and returned in a moment with the book.

Malcolm took it, his eyes on the cowering figure of his mother still twisted sideways to cry into the curve of her arm. When he looked back at Margaret her lip was bitten up between her teeth and her eyes filmed with hot tears. With a swift step he was beside her, had stooped and kissed her thin hard mouth, and then he had lifted Elspeth gently, kissed her too, tasting the salt of her tears. The sight of both these hard old women crying unnerved him, and he choked.

"Good-bye, Mother," he said. "Good-bye, Aunt Margaret."

He started out, but Elspeth leaped to her feet to run after him.

"You'll write, Malcolm? You'll write often?"

"Every week," Malcolm said. "I don't know where I'm going yet,—not to school for a while, anyway,—but I'll write."

Standing in the doorway before the two old women who had brought him up, the old-woman aunt of forty-seven and the equally old-woman mother of forty,—realizing with sentimental, youthful incompleteness the gray imprisonment that their lives must have been, —he wanted to bow his head and weep for the bitterness of their living; but the tears choked him and he turned with a wave of the hand and went out. A few minutes later the two sisters, peering sharp-featured out the window, saw him drive out of the machine shed with Tom Grimmitsch and head out toward the road.

They watched until the car turned right up the hill past Paxleys', and then with something like a sigh they turned to face each other in the empty and depressing house.

In that moment, looking at each other for the third time since Alec's death across the barrier of eighteen gray years, they were sisters again. The cause of their trouble was gone, secure and peaceful in October earth. Malcolm was gone, freed from the grimness of the house he had been born in. The guilt and the shame and the unforgiving and the expiation were gone, and both women knew it as surely as if Margaret had put her arms around Elspeth and said, "Oh, Elspeth, the sword has been drawn between us for so many years, the bitterness and the regret have already taken so much from us, the acid of our wrongs has eaten the love and kindness and lightheartedness out of our lives through so many seasons . . ."

She might have said it—the impulse was there, the barriers weakened by Alec's death and Malcolm's leaving and Elspeth's tears. The jealous hurt and the wrong were shadows of far away and long ago, and the cause of them buried under mounded earth already drifted with October leaves.

But as surely as they knew that they were sisters again, they knew that they were old women. Eighteen years of sunless living lay upon them like a blight, and with Malcolm had gone their last hold upon that life which still knew laughter and a light heart. They were two old women sentenced to the prison they had made for themselves, doomed to wear away slowly, toughly; to fade and wither and dry up inch by inch in the silence of their house.

Their look broke, and Margaret glanced at the locket watch against the flat stiff poplin of her breast.

"We'd best go and straighten up Malcolm's room," she said.

AFTERWORD BY MARY STEGNER

Some time during the year 1936, when my husband was a young English instructor at the University of Utah, he saw an announcement for a Little, Brown and Company novelette prize. At that time he had published only two stories, one in Whit Burnett's *Story* magazine and one in the *Virginia Quarterly Review*. What could he come up with as the subject for a novella? I remembered a family account about my two gaunt aunts who lived with their son in western Iowa. As a young girl I wasn't sure whether the child was the son of the older widowed sister or of the younger spinster sister, but for the purposes of Wally's imagination it didn't really matter what I knew or recalled in detail. From that little seed *Remembering Laughter* grew.

About a year later, on the afternoon of January 31, 1937, Wally received word that he had won the Little, Brown and Company prize of

$2,500 dollars. In those days it was a magnificent sum for a struggling English instructor, and we were, needless to say, overjoyed. Even though I was eight months pregnant we decided to give a party. That night, after great celebration, I went into labor, and thirty hours later produced our only son, Page. Two great events in two days that changed our lives.

Now, nearly sixty years later, Penguin Books is reprinting that first novella, *Remembering Laughter*, a wonderful new addition to the distinguished number of books that Wally was able to give us during a long and astonishingly pro-ductive life.

RECAPITULATION
Bruce Mason returns to Salt Lake City not to perform the perfunct
arrangements for his aunt's funeral but to exorcise the ghosts of his p

ISBN 0-14-02667

REMEMBERING LAUGHTER
In the novel that marked his literary debut, Stegner depicts the drama
moving story of an Iowa farm wife whose spirit is tested by a series
events as cruel and inevitable as the endless prairie winters.

ISBN 0-14-02524

A SHOOTING STAR
Sabrina Castro follows a downward spiral of moral disintegration as
wallows in regret over her dissatisfaction with her older and succes
husband.

ISBN 0-14-02524

THE SOUND OF MOUNTAIN WATER
Essays, memoirs, letters, and speeches, written over a period of twen
five years, which expound upon the rapid changes in the West's cult
and natural heritage.

ISBN 0-14-02667

THE SPECTATOR BIRD
Stegner's National Book Award–winning novel portrays retired lite
agent Joe Allston, who passes through life as a spectator—until he re
covers the journals of a trip he took to his mother's birthplace years bef

ISBN 0-14-01394

WHERE THE BLUEBIRD SINGS TO
THE LEMONADE SPRINGS
Living and Writing in the West
Sixteen brilliant essays about the people, the land, and the art of
American West.

ISBN 0-14-01740

WOLF WILLOW
A History, a Story, and a Memory of the Last Plains Frontier
Introduction by Page Stegner
In a recollection of his boyhood in southern Saskatchewan, Steg
creates a wise and enduring portrait of a pioneer community exis
on the verge of the modern world.

ISBN 0-14-11850